THE HEALER'S HEART

MAIL ORDER STARBRIDES-BOOK 1

BETSY LOVE

THE HEALER'S HEART

Mail Order StarBrides
Book 1

Dedication

***DeWalt*-Always and Forever my happily ever after**
***Joy Love Guenther**-My favorite eldest daughter*

CHAPTER 1

*G*iada had to get off Earth. Now. On a new planet, she could start her life over with a clean slate; one that didn't involve manslaughter – or polygamy. She pressed her back against the side of the glass building and slid to the ground, her heart pounding, her breathing shallow. The bushes and the cover of darkness hid her from the Amahrian enforcers.

The skimmer – a wide walkway running in front of the downtown skyscrapers – normally shuttled the mass of people through the city. Tonight, it carried but a few who were brave enough to face the chilly evening.

A gust of wind picked up a strand of Giada's hair and blew it across her forehead. She tucked it back into her braid and jammed her cold hands into her coat pockets.

The whirring traffic beyond the skimmer hovered in multiple layers, the hover cars lowest, the AeVe – Aero-Vehicle – traffic between, while the distance runners at the top hurried to their destinations. If only Giada could get on a runner heading to the off-world transport without getting caught. She should have grabbed the engagement ring, the one she'd removed when she found out that Lorenzo already had a wife. The diamond alone would have bought her passage to any colonized planet in the galaxy, except that the minute she sold it to purchase an off-world ticket, the Amahrians would trace her faster than she could board the spaceship. She had to find some other way off Earth, one that wouldn't alert the Amahrian League. Getting away from her ex-fiancé was an added benefit.

The enforcers moved on up the street, and Giada breathed out a short huff of relief. Tears burned her eyes.

Lorenzo stepped off the skimmer. He must have parked his AeVe somewhere safe. "Gigi, where are you?"

"Here," she whispered. Now she wished she hadn't agreed to wait for him and his promise of finding a solution to her crime. She had no one else to turn to, not even her coworkers at the clinic could help; not now, not after her offense.

Lorenzo looked far from the confident man she'd known him to be. He'd just witnessed the death of his friend. He hurried across the grass to her and crouched in the bushes, making sure his tailored suit coat didn't touch the ground. "I couldn't take care of the body since his WD signaled his death. You don't have much time until they locate you."

Giada sniffled, the tears threatening to spill.

Lorenzo brushed his thumb under her eye, catching the droplet before it ran down her face. "Hey, it wasn't your fault."

She jerked under his all too familiar touch. "You and I both know that. The Amahrian League –" Giada should never have used her gift outside the clinic. Even worse, it had resulted in Herrick's death. The penalty for that would be too great to bear.

Lorenzo's breath blew out in little puffs as he spoke. "If I had known about his weak heart, I'd have never brought Herrick to you. I thought it was just a cold."

Her heart raced as she thought about Herrick's wife. "I have to call Fayla."

"It'll be better if I tell her."

She pulled her hands from her pockets and stared down at them examining the small ridge between her thumb and forefinger, the mark of a Has'e. A hundred years ago the Amahrians had brought her father's race to earth because of their healing abilities, and then restricted those abilities. Perhaps she should blame the failed healing on her Earther side, the part that was her mother. She shook her head. That couldn't be it either. Giada looked up at Lorenzo. "I'm a good healer. What went wrong?"

"Sometimes these things just happen." Lorenzo took one of her hands and rubbed at her cold fingertips.

She pulled away from Lorenzo. "This never would have happened if I'd insisted we take him to the clinic." Her head fell into her palms. "He didn't seem that ill. One touch, that's all Herrick needed. I've done heals like this plenty of times. He should *not* have gone into cardiac arrest." Giada had a hard time facing the reality that something as simple as a cold had stopped the man's heart.

"No, he shouldn't have."

Giada pinched her lips and clenched her jaw, then rested her head against the cold window pane behind her. "I'll be arrested for killing him. They'll come after you as an accomplice."

Lorenzo cringed and ran his hand down his slacks. "I'll figure it out. But first we need to find somewhere safe for you."

"Where? I can't go back to my flat, the enforcers will be waiting for me there." She couldn't sleep in her AeVe either, not with her GPS tracer on it. And she certainly couldn't go to Lorenzo's apartment, not with his…his…wife. Her lip trembled. She'd been so lonely after Pops died. And then Lorenzo wallied into her life, swept her off her feet. Proposed. How stupid she'd been for not searching him out thoroughly. She thought her troubles with him were over, until he showed up tonight on her doorstep with Herrick. Just a cold. Just a quick heal. And then Herrick would be on his way. And so would Lorenzo.

Lorenzo hung his head. "I'm so sorry about all of this."

Giada turned her back to him for fear she'd start crying all over again. No more tears for this two-timing, lying scuzkit.

"Oh, Gigi." He put his hand on her shoulder. "I wish…I wish I could start over." He almost sounded like he meant it – almost.

Giada shot around to face him. "You don't get to do things over, Lorenzo. You get one shot at life. I've pretty well messed up mine. I suggest you go back to your wife." Pops would tell her she was doing the right thing letting him go. Even Father Universe would concur.

Lorenzo took her by both of her shoulders. As she gazed at his dashing, rugged features and his blond hair with never a lock out of place, she wished he'd never stepped into her life. It would have been easier to continue on with her work and face her loneliness, than to have to suffer the agony of his betrayal.

And now that she'd broken the law, she had no one to turn to, except Lorenzo. She hated that. But what could he do to help her?

He dropped his hand and gazed off across the street. "I have this friend."

Giada waited for him to go on.

"Her name is Elspeth Montgomery. She helps women in desperate situations."

"What kind of help?"

"She can get you off Earth without alerting the Amahrian League. Her terms are a bit unusual." He flicked open his wrist digital.

Giada reached over and snapped his WD closed. "If you use that here, they'll know where we are."

"I put an anti-tracer on it." Lorenzo flipped his WD open again.

"Those are illegal."

"It's okay, I left my real one at home."

Giada clenched her fists; things were moving too fast. She needed time to think. "You can't tell her what happened."

Lorenzo hesitated and dropped his head. "I won't. I'll just tell her you're in a sticky situation with an old lover and need to get off Earth. That at least is the truth." When he looked back at Giada he hesitated a moment before he spoke. "It's the least I can do after all that's happened between us."

Giada wrapped her arms around herself and gritted her teeth. "You better make this work." The ramifications of getting caught hung heavy in her stomach, and she thought she was going to be sick.

CHAPTER 2

The zithar ray hit Skyler with a volt of energy that buckled him to his knees. Every molecule in his body shrank until his shirt sagged like a bilden's skin on his normally muscular frame, and his pants dragged under his footgear, which flopped like grayskirs in a jar. Before he reached the end of the terrace, Paxt caught up to him and slammed the butt of the gun down on his nose. Skyler rolled to the side and held his bridge, trying to stem the flow of blood.

Kaldavia screamed and grabbed her father's arm. "Father, not again."

Paxt hovered over Skyler, the zithar aimed at his face. "I trusted you with my daughter, and this is how you take care of her? You're lucky I've only set it for atmospheric ephemeral."

It wasn't Skyler's fault that Kaldavia had thrown herself at him. Their one and only kiss had been her doing, and truth be told, she slopped it all over his mouth. No, Kaldavia had not managed to capture his heart, either.

Skyler didn't dare argue with her father, especially holding a weapon that had the capability of shrinking him out of existence. Better to pretend he was to blame. "I'm so sorry. I am an imbecile in the ways of the Helexos. It was my mistake assuming that –"

"You have thirty gyrocriks to get off this planet." The whir from Paxt's zithar made it clear if Skyler didn't start running, he'd be shrunken into nothing.

Skyler jumped to his feet and darted around a pillar, tripping over his pant legs. The blast sent several plants wilting into oblivion. Before the weapon could charge again, Skyler leapt over the banister. A dense fern broke his fall. He grabbed his fedora, which had fallen off, and slammed it over his head, tilting it back so he could see, then picking up his pant legs like a lady's long dress, he darted through the trees. He didn't look back to see if Paxt had followed him, nor did he stop when he reached the spaceship docking hanger.

As Skyler passed by a robot on a hoverskien, it called, "Your ship is fueled. Advise you check your electro-heligramix." Skyler barely caught what the maintenance robot said and kept running.

He skirted around a couple of other space craft docked near the exit port where his ship, the Lady Parsec, sat.

His seventeen-year-old nephew stood next to the boarding ramp, thumbing through his WD, looking at holograms of earlier versions of the Parsec P39. "Heyo, Sky." Ceyric didn't look up as he kept flicking through his WD. "You're back early. I was just getting ready to head into town. I wanted to ask about my father."

Each gasp of air burned Skyler's lungs. "We have to go. Now."

Ceyric closed out of his screen. "What happened to you?"

Doubled over, trying to get his breath, Skyler held his hands on his knees. "Zithar."

"Zithar? Aren't those illegal?"

"That's what I thought." Skyler's drooping pants covered his bare feet. He had no idea when he'd lost his shoes. It didn't matter. He didn't intend to spend one more gyrocrick on this planet.

Ceyric pulled one side of his mouth into a lopsided smirk. "I take it wife hunting didn't go so well."

"Nope, not going to find one here, that's for sure."

Ceyric shook his head. "Maybe you're looking in the wrong places. You should follow your mom's advice and try looking in your own backyard."

"Earth?" With the Amahrian's bounty on Skyler, he couldn't spend time there. Prison would make raising a family impossible. "Just so you know, that wasn't my fault, either." Skyler should have just left the marriage brokering to the professionals. He never expected the Amahrian princess to cry *kidnap* when her future husband wasn't to her liking.

Skyler rolled his head back, trying to ease the pain in his neck. "We have to head back to Earth anyway. It's a brief stop. I have cargo I have to pick up."

Ceyric shook his head. "One of these days, I'd really like to stay long enough to see my mom."

"I'd like to see my mother as well." Except that visiting her meant a barrage of pestering. *Have you found the right woman, yet? When are you getting married? I'm not getting any younger. Don't you think I'd like to enjoy my grandchildren while I'm young enough to do so?*

He longed for a family of his own as well. Finding someone from Earth meant Skyler would have to face the penalty if he couldn't prove himself innocent. Skyler drew in a short breath and released it. "I'll have to just keep looking elsewhere."

"I know why you can't find the right woman. You're worried she might not measure up, huh?"

"Now, look, if you're going to start joking about this –" Skyler grabbed his head to try and ease the explosions going on there.

Ceyric wrinkled his brow and bit his lip. "Will you have to stay this way?"

"Kaldavia's father said he set it to atmospheric ephemeral. Which means I should regain my normal size once we leave this planet." Skyler did not look forward to more pain as the effects reversed. He hiked up his pants and stared down at his grotesquely shrunken feet.

"So, if I'm to understand, you'll never come back here again?" Ceyric shook his head.

"Not unless I want to face Paxt's wrath, or look like this." Skyler motioned to Ceyric to follow him up the ramp. "Let's get out of here."

Together they moved up the gangplank, every step agony on Skyler's shrunken body.

"Hello Captain." Lady Parsec's onboard system greeted him.

He managed to croak out, "How fares my ladyship."

"Missing you as always." Her soothing voice took some of the agony from his head.

Ceyric helped him into his captain's chair.

"Weight and mass are the same," Lady said. "However, size decrease has been duly noted."

Ceyric released his hold on Skyler as he slumped into his seat. "He got hit with a zithar."

"Zithar?" Lady asked. "Those have been outlawed since the militia wars of twenty-three forty."

"Tell that to Kaldavia's father." Skyler leaned forward as shots of agony coursed through his joints. The hat had slipped over his brow and blocked his view of the ship's fore-screens.

"That hat. It's shunnishly old fashioned, and doesn't quite match the rest of your suit, or your size." Ceyric scowled, his boyish features so much like his father's.

"Let them shun away..." Skyler paused, realizing Ceyric's normal teasing was absent. "Thinking about your dad?"

Ceyric gave a shrug. "Yeah, kind of. I wanted to ask around. I was hoping someone had seen him."

"I already asked. He was here, but didn't stay long." Skyler understood perfectly the loss of family. First, Skyler's sister, then his dad, and finally, his brother's disappearance.

"I just hope someone didn't shrink him out of existence," Ceyric said.

"I don't think your dad would have run up against an angry father. He was always faithful to your mom."

Ceyric had only been two when Marcus left on a cargo run and never returned. As Ceyric grew up, he told his mother he wanted to be a pilot, just like his dad.

Much to her sorrow, she finally gave in to Ceyric's begging to be Skyler's copilot. If she hadn't, the kid would probably have joined the Amahrian fleet as a wing commander. Flying was in his blood. Just like Marcus. Skyler suspected the only reason she let him go was the hope he'd find his father.

Skyler hoped that as well one day. Changing the subject, he cleared the lump in his throat. "Perhaps the hat will keep the Gitlish diggers away." Skyler pretended to glare. "No short jokes, understood?"

"Me? Short jokes? I'd never stoop to such a level." Ceyric grinned, his features accented by the glint in his eye.

Relieved that Ceyric had returned to his normal self, Skyler pushed his fedora back so he could see out from under the brim. "Very funny." He gripped the armrests. "I am ready to get off this planet, if that's not too *tall* of an order." Skyler gave a sideways glance at Ceyric.

Ceyric chuckled. "Good one."

Once Ceyric sat in his copilot's seat, Lady Parsec remarked, "Ceyric, I see that you have maintained your stature."

"Some things are not worth risking height adjustments." Ceyric turned his glance toward Skyler.

Skyler ignored the remark. "Okay, my lady, engines in take-off operation."

"Destination, Captain?"

"Earth."

Ceyric shook his head and placed his hand on the navigation panel. "Better make it a quick stop. Don't want the Amahrians to find out you're back – you might get the short end of the stick. Oh, wait, you already did."

CHAPTER 3

*L*orenzo took Giada's arm and led her inside a café with dark corners and dingy lighting. She wished she'd had another alternative than accepting help from a stranger, especially from Lorenzo's friend, but she had no other choice.

He pulled a chair out for her at a back table, facing the door. "Here, sit."

Giada perched in the chair, ready to flee at the first sign of an enforcer. "What does Elspeth look like?"

"You'll know her when she comes in." He adjusted his suit collar. "I'd stay, but I have to get home to my wife."

Even in the warmth of the café, she shivered and pulled her coat tighter around her body. "What about Fayla?"

He shook his head. "I'm sure the Amahrians have already contacted her."

"What about you? They'll know you were there." Giada continued to tremble.

"Don't worry about me. I can talk my way out of anything."

"Yeah, you're pretty good at that." He'd certainly done his share of sweet-talking her.

Lorenzo shrugged. "Only order the yousa. Well, you know why…"

Of course she knew why. Yousa was free. Add-ins meant using her sina account, and that would bring enforcers.

"Good luck. I'm so sorry it all turned out like this." He took Giada's hand, and brought it to his lips. Then without a backward glance, he walked out. Instead of being heartbroken, she was relieved.

The robot waiter whirred to her table on his hoverskien. "What can I get for you?"

"Just yousa, thank you."

"Cream, sugar, caramel?" His light blipped as he spoke.

"Just plain."

The robot sped off toward the kitchen.

Giada looked at the screen displaying the menu complete with holographic presentations of the food. Queasy, she flipped off the menu and opened a series of news articles. Scanning them, she looked for anything about Herrick. Of course, it was too soon.

The only thing of interest was a holographic video about the failure of the relocation efforts during the Gridenti invasion, and now years later they were calling for the removal of the chips embedded for family identifications. That would mean a steady stream of patients at the clinic. Too bad she couldn't be there to help in the process. Pops would have approved of their removal. He'd refused to have his family subjected to it.

She went back to scanning and could find nothing about Herrick.

"May I join you?" A woman dressed in ancient clothing interrupted Giada's search.

"Elspeth Montgomery?" The only time Giada had seen a floor length, bustled dress like that was in the museum. She wondered if the woman had attained her tiny waist with an equally antique corset. Her bright blue eyes had the barest of wrinkles around them. Her full lips were turned up in a smile. Giada could only guess at her age – late thirties maybe.

"Pleased to make your acquaintance." Elspeth gave Giada a brilliant smile – her teeth whiter than any she'd ever seen. Elspeth picked up her long skirt and slid into the seat on the other side of the table. Her hair billowed out in curls under her bowl-shaped bonnet. The brilliant blue ribbon matched the dress's sash and buttons and made her eyes sparkle like sapphires.

Giada continued to stare at the woman who had stepped out of a history digital.

The waiter whirred to the table with two narrow mugs of yousa. He set one in front of each of them. Steam rose in gentle swirls from the top. How had the waiter known he'd be serving two? Giada pulled her brows together.

"Are you ready to order?" the waiter asked.

Elspeth took a sip of her yousa. "Give us a minute?"

The waiter whirred off.

Elspeth's smile did nothing to comfort Giada. "Now then, Lorenzo said you need to get off Earth."

Lorenzo's communication to Ms. Montgomery had been rather vague, so Giada wondered how much she should tell this woman about her situation. Elspeth may decide not to help her once she discovered how much trouble Giada was in. "Well, it's...difficult to explain."

"I am always discreet." Elspeth laid her gloved hand on Giada's arm. "You're not the first young woman I've helped out of a sticky situation."

Giada pinched her lips together trying to decide if she could trust Elspeth.

An enforcer strode through the door and Giada slumped down in her chair. He walked to the counter and examined the replicator before punching in his selection.

"There, there." Elspeth patted Giada's hand. "I understand." She left the table and sauntered to the enforcer, her dress swishing as she went. "Replicator food never quite tastes the same as the real thing, does it?"

The enforcer's brow shot up and his nostrils flared with their gill-like opening. "No, it doesn't." He looked down to where Elspeth was stroking his arm.

"I know this place around the corner. Their food is simply delicious." The brim of Elspeth's bonnet bobbed as she spoke. "Let me buy you dinner."

"Oh, no, I couldn't let you do that." He pulled his webbed hand from Elspeth's touch and rubbed it over his hairless head. "Thank you for your kind offer, but this is really quicker."

"Then won't you join me here?"

Join her here? What was Elspeth thinking? Giada slumped down farther. She could no longer see the enforcer around Elspeth.

"I'm on duty. But thank you for your offer." The Amahrian grabbed his selection and hurried out the door.

Elspeth crossed the room and slid back into her seat. "You just have to know how to scare them off." She stroked Giada's arm the same way she'd done with the enforcer. "Just like that."

"Oh." Giada pulled her hand back, Elspeth's touch creepy against her skin.

"Now then, where were we?"

"I have to get off Earth. My fiancé –" Giada caught herself. "I mean my ex-fiancé and I were supposed to be married. Four days is all we had left. His wife sent me a communication –"

"I can imagine how heartbreaking that must have been." Elspeth smiled again. "But that's not why you want to get off Earth, is it?"

Giada shook her head.

"Enforcer problems?"

Giada nodded. "Oh, please, can you help me?"

Elspeth sat back as if contemplating. "I can, but you understand that passage is very expensive.

Giada jumped in. "I can repay you."

Elspeth gave a nervous chuckle. "You do realize that the minute I accept your sinas, I become an accomplice to whatever crime it is you committed?

That did pose a huge problem. "How will I ever repay you?"

"You can, but not in the way you are thinking. I'll explain it all in a moment." Elspeth motioned for the waiter. "But first, I'm famished, and I'm sure you are as well."

"I can't access my account at all, can I?"

"You won't need to. It's all covered." Elspeth flipped out of the news feed on the table digital and pulled up the menu. "You should try the braised beef. It's simply to die for."

"Braised beef?" Giada had never heard of such a thing.

"That's right. Here it's called Brawn Tew." She turned to the robot. "Bring us two of your most tender Tew."

"Two Tender Tew for Two." He blipped and whirred away.

Giada raised an eyebrow and frowned. "I've never been able to afford Tew."

"Oh, don't worry. A lovely gentleman is splurging on us tonight." Elspeth leaned back and took another sip of her yousa.

"Who would want to pay for my meal?"

"Let's just say that this is part of the bargain to get you off Earth." Elspeth tilted her head to the side, a smug look on her face. "Now then, after we finish our meal, we'll find more comfortable surroundings, and I'll tell you all about your future free of enforcers."

CHAPTER 4

Skyler navigated Lady Parsec onto a dried meadow under cover of darkness far from the Amahrian outpost. "Good thing we were able to reinitiate the stealth order on her, eh?"

"Yes, but don't let anyone know we're here. Let's just get in and get your cargo before the Amahrians find out." Ceyric slid his hand over the control panel. The lights in the cockpit dimmed as the side ramp slid down.

Skyler pulled his flight jacket around his shoulders. "I have to get to the rendezvous point before midnight. I'll be back in a crik." The jacket still sagged a bit, but at least he no longer looked like a dwarf. His feet managed to fill his extra pair of deck shoes.

"I really wish you had told me what the cargo is. Can I at least know how heavy it is so I can calibrate a swift take-off in case we run into trouble?"

"Light, actually. No calibration needed." Skyler strode to the ramp. "Not more than one ninety kilos if it's as hefty as the last one. If it's a light one, not less than forty kilos."

"You're not smuggling criminals, are you?" Ceyric followed Skyler. "Oh, wait. Not another Amahrian princess who wants to leave Earth because her father is a dictator."

"Neither. And that reference to Islae isn't funny either." Skyler couldn't help it if the match didn't work out, and Islae had sent that communication to her father. No, this cargo had already been bought and paid for.

With a shake of his head, he stepped into the meadow, the dried grass crunching under his feet. Too bad he hadn't arrived during the rainy season. He missed the smell of wet grass, Earth grass.

"Okay, so, tell me what the cargo is. I hate not knowing." Ceyric shuffled his foot.

"The less you know until we take off, the better." Skyler headed off across the meadow towards the city lights. Ah, it was good to be back on Earth, even if the Amahrians wanted his head in a kryler. The whole incident had been a misunderstanding. He just couldn't face what they'd do to him.

If Madam Montgomery hadn't sent that interstellar message, he would have stayed as far away as possible. Her offer had been far too lucrative to resist. Shipping starbrides paid well, and this one doubled what he'd gotten for the last three combined.

Skyler pulled a dark cloak from his pack and tied it around his neck. With each breath, the effects of the zithar wore off, and his belt crimped tight around his waist. He unfastened it and redid it to its usual notch. That was a bit better, but the pain in his joints from returning to normal still slowed his movements. Another reason to get in, grab his cargo, and get out. He didn't think he'd have the endurance for what a kryler might do to him.

In the sky above him, the stars danced in their brilliance. Since the cities had adopted the pluerial rays in their lighting systems, the night universe looked as it must have before the invention of the electric bulb. In spite of their governing style, the Amahrians had brought technology that had saved the dying planet. It had taken almost two hundred years to repair the damage humankind had inflicted.

Once Skyler reached the outskirts of town, he pulled the hood over his head and kept it down in case anyone caught site of his face. Several AeVe cars sped along magnetic tracks, oblivious to a lone pedestrian. At the first transport station he came to, he exchanged a token through the sina port. He hoped his coin would keep him anonymous, keep the Amahrians from figuring out he was back on Earth.

An enforcer sat at the front of the transport, his face in his wrist digital, fingers flicking through the screens. His gills puffed in and out on the sides of his flattened nose.

Skyler kept his head down as if what was on his WD fascinated him. He tried to concentrate on an article about changes being made to the League of Federations and the impact of interstellar trade. Luckily, his cargo didn't fall under the new regulations. While the Amahrian system of exports, tariffs and government wasn't perfect, it certainly worked better than the old Earth one.

At least the Amahrians didn't stick their gills into every aspect of life, and they'd managed to clean up the atmosphere.

He took a deep breath and scanned his digital. Then switched to the time stamp icon – Twenty-three fifty-two. His cargo should be ready by about now. He hoped this one was as easy and eager to get off earth as the last three.

The transport stopped at the platform several stories below Elspeth's apartment. The Amahrian looked up and gave Skyler a slight nod. Skyler pulled the hood closer to his face and nodded back as he stepped off the transport onto the platform. A puzzled look crossed the Amahrian's face. Skyler hoped he hadn't been recognized from the hologram that showed up on countless enforcer's digitals.

As the transport left the platform, the Amahrian pressed his hands against the glass, his nose flattened even more, as he tried to get a closer look. Skyler would have to grab his cargo and get back to the ship before the enforcer could figure out who he'd had the privilege of sharing a ride with.

CHAPTER 5

The elevator doors opened at the thirty-second floor. Giada followed Elspeth down a long hallway with plush carpet. She stopped in front of a door marked Madam Montgomery, Procurer of Fine Commodities and Oddities.

Elspeth swiped her hand over the security scanner and waited for the door to open. She hadn't discussed Giada's future since leaving the restaurant, insisting that Giada accompany Elspeth back to her apartment.

Giada kept telling herself the only reason she agreed to go to Elspeth's apartment was the hope of getting off Earth. A warm place to sleep for tonight was an added benefit.

As they entered the spacious room, Giada left the modern world behind. It was like stepping into a page from her history digital.

"Wow." She couldn't help but be amazed. From the brocade couches to the parasol made of silk to the china in the hutch, everything dated back to before the twentieth century.

"You like?" Elspeth removed her gloves and set them on an end table.

"It's fabulous." Giada studied an eighteenth-century painting. "Is it an original?"

"I wish. Sadly, everything here is a replica." Elspeth motioned down a short hall. "Follow me, please."

Giada entered another room furnished with a bed sporting four carved pieces of wood. The cover over the mattress had tiny stitches close together, the pattern did not match the intricate squares of the fabric. She touched the thick material, so different from her myralin blankets.

Elspeth stood behind her. "In there is the bath. I'm sure you'd like to soak."

"Soak? Soak what?" Giada peeked into the bathroom.

"Your body. Come, I'll show you."

The bathroom was unlike anything Giada had ever seen. Nowhere was there an electronic ablution. Instead, a large container on short golden feet with odd looking knobs took prominence in the room. The creamy inside set off the black exterior. Giada swallowed.

Elspeth crossed to the container and turned two of the knobs. Water poured out of them. From a shelf over the tub, she took a glass bottle and poured a purple liquid into the water. Bubbles expanded until they formed a thick layer of frothy foam. "Now, remove your clothes and get into the bathtub. And when I come back, we'll discuss your future."

"What?" Giada eyed the substance in the tub and backed away.

"Oh, you poor, sweet thing." Elspeth put an arm around Giada's shoulder. "I can only imagine what you've been through." She gave Giada's arm a light pat. "I promise this will help to calm your nerves. The bubbles have real lavender extract and a few other soothing additives. It's designed to relax both body and spirit. You'll never want to get out." She pulled the stopper from the glass bottle. "Here, take a good whiff."

Unsure, Giada took a quick sniff. The heavenly aroma enveloped her and the room took on a hazy glow.

"There now, see?" Elspeth corked the bottle. "I use this all the time. It's better than any drug you can find out there, and it has no lingering side effects. Now then, you relax, and I'll be right back, then we'll discuss your future." She left the room.

Elspeth was right; Giada's heart no longer raced, and euphoria settled over her. As the aroma continued to waft around her, she undressed and stepped into the tub, allowing the foam to surround her as she sank into the water. Whatever was in the mixture alleviated her anxiety.

Elspeth entered again with two fluffy pink towels. One she hung over the edge of the tub, just out of reach of the water. The other she draped over a bar. "You must have had a rough time of it. It's not necessary for you to tell me everything, but I do need to ask you a few questions. You already told me about your involvement with Lorenzo. That surely isn't why you want to get off Earth."

Giada clenched her jaw. "No." If her father had only lived long enough to have warned her about Lorenzo. "I did something pretty bad."

Elspeth perched on the edge of a small stool. "Something that involves Amahrian laws?"

Giada nodded. "I'm afraid if I tell you what it is, you won't want to help me."

Elspeth chuckled. "Oh, my dear. If you only knew some of the reasons women want to leave Earth, you'd probably think your situation is trivial."

How could being responsible for someone's death be considered trivial?

"What would you say if I told you I'd killed a man."

"Did you mean to?"

"No!" Giada's gift was to heal. "It wasn't supposed to happen. Actually, it's not his death that's the problem, it's where he died."

Elspeth nodded thoughtfully. "I see."

"It is bad, isn't it? And you'll be in so much trouble for helping me." Tears tipped the edge of her lids and disappeared into the bubbles.

"It does pose a problem, but not significantly." Elspeth untied the ribbons and laid the bonnet in her lap. "If I had a way to get you off Earth, would you be interested? You'll never have to face enforcers. You'll never have to worry about money ever again. And the best part is that you will find love."

"Love?"

"Let me tell you about the man who paid for your meal this evening." Elspeth pulled up her WD. "He communicated with me about needing a wife."

"Wife? I don't have any intention of getting married." Giada would have slammed her fists down into the water if she hadn't been so relaxed.

"Just hear me out." Elspeth smoothed an imaginary wrinkle. "My business is connecting brides and grooms to their perfect matches."

Something about her statement jiggled a memory. "You're a modern-day marriage broker." Before the twentieth century, an unmarried man would use the old mail system and order a bride.

A quick nod followed Elspeth's smile. "You're starting to get the picture."

Giada leaned back again, letting the bubbles swirl around her. "So, if I agree to be some man's wife on another planet, he'll pay for my passage?" A ray of possibility shone in her imagination. But marriage? She didn't know how she could do that. "How soon do I have to give you an answer?"

The smile left Elspeth's face as she lowered her brows. "Here's my dilemma. You see, there's a cargo ship waiting for you right now."

"For me?"

"Yes. The woman who was supposed to board that ship has gotten cold feet. It's of mutual benefit to both of us."

When Giada had pictured getting off Earth, never in a millennia did she consider the option of being a starbride. If she didn't like the man, she could always find employment and repay him for her passage. "Tell me about him."

"He lives on Jesighe. He's a widower. His wife was a tender woman with incredible compassion, and stood beside him as he serves in his position of governor to the imperial city of Takolohi. He has a great deal of power and wealth. You will never want for anything. All he asks is that you stand beside him, fulfil the duties of a governor's wife. And by mutual consent, you will keep his bed warm."

"I have to have sex with a perfect stranger?" Giada's hands grew cold as her face grew hot. "I...I can't...do that." Of course, he'd want sex. That's what being married entitled. But with someone she didn't know?

"We all start out as perfect strangers, dear. He will not rush you. You will have plenty of time to get to know each other. Perhaps you might even grow to love one another. He wants someone who will give him her heart. He wants a Has'e."

"How do you know I'm Has'e?" Giada asked.

Elspeth's eyes shifted to her bonnet. "Lorenzo told me."

It was quite a coincidence that the woman who'd back out was Has'e as well.

Elspeth interrupted her thoughts. "Do you think you could give him your heart?"

"Any love I had in my heart, my ex-fiancé destroyed." Giada brought her knees up and wrapped her arms around them.

A fleeting look of shock crossed Elspeth's face. "Did you give Lorenzo your heart?"

"Lorenzo? I never said who I was engaged to."

"Oh." Elspeth gave a nervous chuckle. "I just assumed, well, because, I know how he operates. We've been..." She paused and picked at imaginary lint on her bonnet. "Shall we say...acquaintances for many years. But you did say you did not give him your heart, didn't you?"

"Absolutely, not."

Elspeth clasped her hands. "Thank goodness."

"Why do you say that?" Giada pulled her eyebrows together.

Elspeth leaned forward. "As a Has'e you know the significance of giving your heart."

Of course, Giada understood. Pops explained it often over the course of her teen and throughout her adult years. When a Has'e gives her heart, a metaphysical change occurs and she is bonded forever to him. Pops also made it clear that it should never happen before marriage. Her father made her promise to guard her heart.

But could she give it to a complete stranger? Giada considered her options. Homeless and on the run from the government. Orphaned.

Jobless. Not to mention what Lorenzo had done to her. "This man on Jesighe – he'll give me all the time I need?" Giada felt a lump form in her throat and slide deep into her chest. "He'll wait for me to give him my heart?"

Elspeth nodded. "His name is Alem Balek."

"Do you have a picture of him?"

Elspeth held out her wrist digital as Giada leaned over the rim of the tub.

A hologram of a black haired, broad nosed, dark skinned man popped up. His face looked both handsome and kindly.

"He's a Polynesian Earther." Giada gazed into his chocolate eyes.

"Yes, and he wants an Earth bride. And how lucky he will be to get a Has'e."

"Half Has'e. My mother was an Earther." Giada bit the inside of her lip. "Did you do a background check on him? He's not violent, is he?"

"I never send my brides to men who are not thoroughly inspected beforehand." Elspeth's voice rose in pitch as if no one ever questioned her. "Look, he even sent you a letter."

"To me?"

"Well, not to you specifically, but to the one he hoped would be his bride." She held the WD closer so that Giada could read the communication.

It began:

Dearest Bride,

How lonely I have been here since the passing of my sweet wife. I have loved her and honored her. I have proven to be a good husband and provider. The sun has set on our union, but I know that she smiles down upon me. Her last words before she passed from this place were, "Find another for you to love as you have loved me, my precious. Lucky is the woman who finds strength in your arms."

I do not say this to boast of myself, but to prove to you, my wondrous, brave woman who embarks on such an adventure across the galaxies, that you will be cherished and lavished as is deserving of the wife of a governor.

I await your arrival, and pray that you will have safety in your journey.

Anxious to love again,

26

Alem Balek

Certainly a cruel man's wife would not sing his praises. She studied the man's image again. Pops said that you could tell the soul of a man by his eyes. Alem Balek appeared to be as he said.

"He is a pillar of integrity in his community. In all the background checking our company did on behalf of his bride, we could find nothing amiss."

Pops, what should I do? Giada closed her eyes waiting for him to answer.

On the table where Giada had put her things, her WD vibrated. A hologram signaling an incoming message from Lorenzo popped up. "The enforcers came by my home before I got there. My wife said they're now searching for you."

Giada glanced again at the image of Alem Balek on Elspeth's WD, her heart pounding in her chest. "It looks like I have no other option."

"Wonderful." Elspeth clapped her hands together. "I'll gather some things together for you. You don't want to meet him looking as you do. I'd already packed a traveler for his bride. Since you're the exact same size, I'm sure you'll find some pretty clothing to your liking." Elspeth ran a hand along her coiffed hair. Giada almost fell asleep listening to Elspeth tell her all about the duties Giada would have as wife to the most prominent man on Jesighe.

"Here." Elspeth brought Giada from her reverie and handed her another purple container. "While I gather a few more things together, you should wash with that lavender cleanser. You'll love what it does for your hair."

Giada sunk down, letting the warm water surround all but her face.

To think, this morning she'd never dreamed she'd be getting married, let alone to a complete stranger.

CHAPTER 6

Skyler hit his foot boosters and zipped up to Elspeth's apartment on the thirty-second floor. He landed on her balcony, barely missing several potted plants holding strawberry azaleas. Tonight, he did not have time to indulge in their fragrance. He gave three sharp raps on the glass window. If he used the identification pad, the Amahrian enforcers would know his exact location. He'd already risked being located when he used the transport. As it was, it wouldn't take long for the enforcer on the transport to figure out Skyler Rohn was back on Earth. Soon, he'd have a whole squad after him. Hopefully his cargo didn't carry a lot of baggage so he could make a quick getaway.

Shifting from foot to foot, he waited for Elspeth to answer his knock. He shrugged under his still drooping flight jacket. At least Ceyric hadn't suggested he'd gotten what he deserved. Next time Skyler needed to look for a wife, he'd make sure she was an orphan. Maybe Elspeth could find a match for him. But then the wife of a space pilot was an awfully lonely position. Mulling over his options, he considered his mother's advice to come back to Earth and fix his mistake. She had no idea what the ramifications would be if he did.

He tapped again. What was taking so long for her to answer?

The balcony door finally slid open. "Skyler Rohn, so good to see you once more. I assume you're late because you had trouble with enforcers again."

"You know I like to come through windows." He took one more look over the balcony before entering her apartment. "Actually, one of them spotted me on the transport. Don't know if he recognized me or not."

"You know, all you have to do is go to the League and explain what happened." Elspeth proffered her hand.

"Well, then, I'll just wally right over to their compound and turn myself in. And then how will we collect?" He knew she wouldn't allow him to do that, especially with all they had riding on this starbride's successful delivery.

"You're positively right, my dear." Elspeth fluttered her hand at him. "Unless, of course, you married me."

Skyler took her hand and gave it a quick kiss. "Who wouldn't want to be your second husband?" He'd never considered Elspeth as wife material, but it didn't hurt to flirt with the woman who paid his wages. And the woman did love a good romance. That had to be why she'd chosen to be a match-maker – to live vicariously through the lives of lonely women desperately seeking true love.

Elspeth sighed. "I see you're still wearing my late husband's fedora."

"I am never without it. Although, I must say, it doesn't do well under a hooded cloak. And it lost its perfect fit when I encountered an angry father with a zithar." Skyler removed his hat and spun it on his finger before tossing it onto an antique hat rack.

"You're lucky you didn't disappear, altogether." She raised her eyebrow. "Your head was always too big for your own good." Elspeth gave the lock of hair that insisted on hanging over his forehead a quick tug.

Skyler pushed the piece of hair back, but it flopped forward again. Using the window as his mirror, he twisted the errant strand around his finger and tucked it under another dark curl.

Elspeth's view out the floor to ceiling windows brought one of the most coveted vistas in all of New Haven. The stars twinkled against an inky sky. Their brilliance, set apart from the city lights, still took his breath away. It didn't matter that he flew among the galaxies, there was something about this view from earth that made him ache to come home for good.

He took in one more glance, memorizing the unique way Orion's belt cinched up and how Taurus settled over Orion's shoulder. How different they looked out in space when they lost the perspective of Earth. Skyler turned back to Elspeth where she stood in the middle of her ancient furnishings.

The most incredible technologies existed on Earth and yet, she insisted in living with her relics of the past.

Elspeth crossed to the food panel. "Yousa." At least she indulged in a few modern conveniences. The machine whirred and dropped a cylinder full of the steamy liquid. "Skyler?" she asked.

"Nothing for me." He paced the floor, stopping to glance into Elspeth's bedroom. "So where is this cargo you wanted me to ship?"

Before her yousa finished brewing, Elspeth turned to eye him. "One does not ship a bride. One carries a starbride like a delicate feather for a bonnet. Will you please stop referring to my girls as cargo?"

"I get paid to transport. That's all I care about." Skyler moved to the window again.

A transport pulled up on the landing platform a few stories below. Three enforces along with two robot guards disembarked. The RGs eyes blinked orange, signaling stun level. They spread out in several directions, one of them entering the corridor.

Elspeth joined him at the window, sipping from her cup. "It's a good thing you came in from my balcony entrance."

"Where is my cargo?"

Elspeth scowled. "She's taking a bubble bath, if you must know."

"Bubble what?" Skyler backed away from the window.

"You fill a tub full of steamy water and add some liquid bubbles and stir until frothy, never mind that I had to have them specifically made so that complete relaxation takes over the brain. You soak in the fragrant foam to rid yourself of tension."

"She has to do that now?" Skyler made for the bathroom door.

Elspeth intercepted Skyler and placed a hand on his arm. "You can't go in there. She's not dressed, and I told you, she's soaking. After the day she's had, she needed to be relaxed so I could soothe her worries."

"She doesn't have time to soak." Skyler wriggled away from her, crossed to her exterior door and peered out the two-way mirror into the hallway. "They haven't reached this floor yet." He turned back to Elspeth, who casually sipped her yousa as if she had all the time in the universe.

"You still park your Spitfire here?" he asked.

"Of course."

Skyler strode to her, removed the cup from her hands and set it in the dispensary. "Go get the AeVe started."

"I wasn't done with that."

Skyler pushed her toward her garage. "You can make another one after I get my cargo."

Elspeth rolled her eyes. "I told you, she is *not* cargo."

Skyler gave Elspeth a shove in the direction of her garage "Your bride, and my cargo, are not going to get shipped anywhere if we don't leave now."

With a heavy humph, Elspeth passed her hand over the garage panel.

Skyler raced to the bathroom and flung the door open. He had no idea what to expect when Elspeth had said bubble bath. A long container covered in some ancient and slick material sat against the far wall. All he could see were mounds of bubbles and one very pale crown of hair sticking out at one end of the water container.

He scratched his head. "Are you my package?"

The girl screamed and slunk down lower. "Get out!"

"We have to go now; the enforcers are here." He grabbed the towel and held it out to her.

She stood, snatched the towel, and wrapped it around herself carefully so he couldn't see her naked body. Her beauty mesmerized him. The cloth accentuated her shapely body. Bubbles still clung to her skin and danced in her hair. Skyler's eyes traveled up the length of her curves and rested on her face. Her pale blue eyes set against her champagne skin and blonde hair made her look fragile, like one of the glass dolls on Elspeth's shelf. Color rose in the woman's cheeks as he stood staring at her – like strawberries that matched her full lips.

Elspeth burst through the door. "What in heaven's name is going on in here?"

Skyler pulled his gaze away and pointed at the girl. "Your cargo is being uncooperative. And she's wet. I can't take her on board like that."

"Her name is Giada Hallspring. And how many times do I have to tell you, she is *not* cargo." Elspeth grabbed another towel off the wall rack and put it over the top of Giada's head and pressed the fluffy thing against her hair.

At this rate, it would take hours for her to dry off.

"Open up." A deep robotic voice called from outside the apartment. "We're looking for a fugitive." Giada's rosy cheeks lost their delightful glow and her body trembled.

Elspeth pushed Skyler aside and turned back to Giada. "Grab the bags on my bed, dearie. There's a change of clothes in there. You can put them on in the AeVe." Giada nodded and ran into the other room.

With her hand cupped over her mouth Elspeth hollered at the RG. "One second, I'm not dressed." She turned back to Skyler. "I'll stall them."

The voice became more urgent. "Ms. Montgomery, open the door."

"What do you want me to do with your AeVe?" Skyler pulled Elspeth into the hall, passing Giada who still clung to her towel.

"Leave it in the field; I'll collect it tomorrow." Elspeth reached behind her and with deft fingers unfastened her dress.

"How will you explain your missing vehicle?" Skyler asked.

"It's not the first time a rogue like you has taken off with my Spitfire and abandoned it somewhere…shall we say…safe." Elspeth shook her finger at him. "Now, don't mess this up. My client has paid a great deal for a Has'e. Her complexion alone gets us double. And with her healing abilities we're getting quite a pretty sina for this one. Do you understand me?"

Before Skyler could answer, the enforcer pounded again on the door.

"Can you let a lady get dressed first?" Elspeth called back. She handed Skyler her ID chip, and he tucked it in his pocket.

Giada entered the room carrying two bags. A plush robe draped around her. Since she was taller than Elspeth, the robe barely hit her knees and sagged around her slender frame.

Elspeth pushed them both toward the garage. "Now, go."

He took one of the bags from his cargo, grabbed her free hand, and dragged her to the landing bay. The banging at the door grew more intense.

"Madam Montgomery, we shall use safety protocols if you do not open up immediately."

"Coming." She called over her shoulder.

Skyler closed the bay door and inserted the chip into the reader of the Spitfire's panel. Both driver and passenger sides swung open. Skyler threw both of the girl's bags into the vehicle.

Frustrated that his cargo hadn't moved, Skyler slapped the top of the cherry red AeVe. "Don't just stand there. Get in!"

With the robe wrapped tight around her, Giada slipped into the seat.

The AeVe lurched forward and they catapulted over the side and glided past the Amahrian transport.

"Hang on, Honey." Skyler took his eye off the road for a brief moment and glanced at Giada's terrified face. Narrowly missing the building in front of him, he thought, *Don't damage the goods.*

CHAPTER 7

*G*iada gripped the seat and her robe at the same time. Change in the AeVe with a madman driving? What was Elspeth thinking? At least she'd managed to get her under clothes on before Skyler whisked her off. She'd be lucky to get out of this alive. She could hear the report now. Woman's half-naked body found charred in the remains of a Spitfire, at least that's what kind of AeVe she thought it was. She had to be completely insane. That was it. When she'd agreed to be a starbride, this was not what she'd expected.

"Hang on." Skyler practically flipped the AeVe on its side to get around a building, throwing Giada against his shoulder. She clutched the robe tighter as her wet hair flung across her face.

The madman righted the vehicle, hit the accelerator and they soared over the top of several shorter buildings. He must realize those kind of maneuvers were not only dangerous, but illegal.

The AeVe swooped down the back side and glided through a narrow street only used by recyclers. The cubes of compacted materials sat in neat rows, ready to be picked up. Skyler slowed and turned off the running lights as he eased the vehicle between two stacks of trash.

"All right, you can get dressed now."

Giada stared at him. Right here with him watching? She shook her head and motioned for him to turn away. She would have preferred him not gawking at her like he'd done when he watched her get out of the bathtub.

After making sure Skyler had turned toward the window, she pulled a slick pair of pants out of the bag at her feet and shoved her legs into them. The way they clung to the her when she slid them over her hips didn't help. She slid her arms free of Elspeth's robe to pull on the loose top. It slipped easily over her head, and hung off one shoulder.

"Done?" Skyler turned back just as she put her arm through the sleeve.

Giada nodded.

"I thought so." He pointed to the glass.

Her mouth fell open. That scoundrel had watched her the whole time. She flattened her hand and struck him across his face. She hoped his cheek stung as much as her hand.

Skyler reached up and rubbed the red finger prints welling up on his face. "I didn't deserve that."

"Yes you did and a whole lot more." Giada crossed her arms over her chest as if to hide what he'd already seen.

"What did you say?" Skyler stared hard at Giada.

"I said, "That and a whole lot more, you maniac." The man was deaf as well as a scuzkit.

"I know what you said. It's just that – have you done any auto-mated voice responses? You know, like for digitals or say spacecraft?"

"No. I have not." Giada reached into her bag and pulled out a brush and tried to untangle her wet hair.

"You just sound a lot like –" He broke off and shook his head. "I'll just have to let you hear for yourself."

Giada had no idea what he was talking about. Since he'd managed to ruin her bath before she set off across the universe, she just wanted the rest of the journey to be in peace. However, sitting in the dark with the lights dimmed gave her little hope of an uneventful voyage.

Maybe once they left the atmosphere, things would settle down. Her stomach hoped so as well.

She slipped her boots on and buckled them. "That was awfully close with that enforcer. I can't afford a run-in."

"That makes two of us." Skyler leaned forward and stared out the front window.

"What do you mean?" Her stomach lurched at the thoughts of being in an AeVe with a criminal.

"If you must know, the whole thing is not my fault. I just don't have time to get tied up in court at the moment." He leaned to the side and scanned the area next to them. "I'll get it straightened out as soon as I get my cargo – I mean – you to Jesighe."

"Just how long are we going to sit here?" She touched the panel near the viewport and a lighted mirror scrolled down.

"Until the enforcers think we've gotten away." Skyler turned the dim interior lights to dark, his face disappearing in the shadows.

She was glad she didn't have to look at him. A pretty face did not make a stellar man. Except for Pops. Giada smiled. The first one she'd been able to conjure since she'd discovered Lorenzo was married.

"What's that for?" Skyler asked.

"What?"

"You smiled."

Giada turned her head and looked out her window at the square piles. Her smile faded. "Thinking about somebody."

He reached over and touched the lighted mirror making it disappear back into the roof, leaving the interior completely dark. "Ah, your future husband?" Giada noted the mockery in his voice.

"No." She leaned her forehead against the glass and sighed. "If you must know, I'm thinking about the only decent man I've ever known."

An Amahrian robot scooter buzzed close by, its search light scanning the alley farther down.

"Shh…" Skyler touched her arm. Whispering he leaned in closer to her, his breath warm on her cheek, his hand firm on her arm. "They'll find us here for sure."

She gasped and pulled away from his warmth. "I can't get caught."

"You don't look like the kind of woman who gets tangled with the Amahrian government." Skyler had not removed his hand.

"I'm not. And if I had any sense, I'd...I..." She didn't know what she'd do.

"Turn yourself in?" He shook his head and released her arm. "Honey, I've already collected half my money to deliver you."

When she reached for the panel to open the door, Skyler pulled her back.

"I'm not a piece of property to be bought and sold." Giada snapped her head around.

"Yes..." He paused.

The light of the scooter came closer. Giada pressed her lips together and inhaled in fright. "Can we please just get out of here."

"And the sooner the better." Skyler hit the lights, and the AeVe shot straight up and zipped past the scooter.

They rounded a gazebo with a robot band playing an old-fashioned number. The whir from the engine caused them to pause. The enforcer passed through the gazebo making the robots topple on their hoverskiens only to right themselves again.

Two more scooters joined the pursuit. Giada gripped the armrest. Working in a trauma hospital, she'd seen far too many injuries from AeVe accidents. Even with all the safety protocols installed in modern AeVes, humans still broke when malfunctions happened.

"Hold on." Skyler shouted. He hit the speed burner and the AeVe shot straight up the side of a tall building, a maneuver that was never supposed to be used inside city limits.

Far below them, one of the scooters slammed into the wall and burst into flames. The other followed them part way up until gravity pulled it back down.

Giada's stomach lurched, and if it hadn't been several hours since she'd eaten last, she might have covered the rear window in Tew. Even though the scooters held robots, the penalties and fines for their destruction were adding up against them.

Once they reached the top of the building they skimmed across the mirrored surface and jetted out into the open sky, leaving the metropolis lights behind them and the night sky brilliant with its dazzling stars.

Giada released her grip on the armrest and leaned her head back. Her stomach did a flip-flop as if she'd been turned upside down on a whirly-gig. Once the motion of the AeVe stabilized, she closed her eyes and breathed, the scent of something indefinable filled the cabin. She must have been too anxious to have noticed it before. It reminded her a little of how her father smelled when he'd come home from being in the forest, yet there was something else mixed in, sweet and salt at the same time, like caramel.

"That wasn't so bad." Skyler pressed the panel and the window slid open, the night air stealing the fragrance away.

Giada shook her head, letting the wind whip her wet hair around her face. "Just get me to Jesighe."

"That will be a lot easier once we're off Earth."

That was the first thing he'd said that she agreed with. Giada turned to examine her escort. She chose not to think of him as a slave-trader or cargo master. He was simply doing his job. His square jaw silhouetted against the sky, and his dark curls shot out in all directions from his head. They looked soft in the starlight. She almost wanted to run her hands through them. How different they'd feel from Lorenzo's spiked blond hair.

Several years ago, a black man had come into the emergency room where Giada had been working. His curls were tighter. She'd been an apprentice at the time and hadn't resisted the urge to touch the man's head. Skyler's were looser, like the fur on a poogle.

Skyler glanced at her and then back to the field in front of them. "See anything you like?"

Embarrassed, Giada faced forward. "Yes, the sky is really lovely tonight."

Skyler chuckled, and Giada wished he hadn't caught her staring at him.

CHAPTER 8

*E*lspeth's AeVe shuddered as it landed in the grass next to Skyler's Lady Parsec. He scanned the area, relieved the enforcers hadn't followed them here. He opened the doors and jumped from his seat. "Ah, my lady, that didn't take long at all, did it?" he said to Lady Parsec.

"Two hours, sixteen minutes, and twenty-two seconds," Lady Parsec replied. "Not a record, but faster than the last time."

Ceyric came down the upper ramp. "I'll bet your delay was the result of a run in with an Amahrian?"

"Nothing I couldn't handle." Skyler touched the side of the ship. "Any sign of them here?"

"Nope, been too quiet." Ceyric's gaze rested on Giada. "Now there's a look."

Lady Parsec chimed in. "Physical appearance denotes Has'e, fairer than your last starbride. Slender, fifty kilos, no weight adjustment needed. I hope you are not mesmerized by this one."

"Nothing could draw my favor away from you, love." Skyler patted her hull. "And for your information, I was not mesmerized."

"As you say," Lady answered.

Ceyric rolled his eyes. "Gibbets, you'd think you were having an affair with your ship."

Skyler gave Ceyric a quick slap on the back and whispered, "Just to keep her happy." Skyler turned to Giada and motioned to his copilot. "Ceyric Rohn, my nephew. Giada Hallspring."

"So you're a starbride?" Ceyric took Giada's bags as she tried to wrestle them from the AeVe. "Never met one before. What's it like to do something so crazy?"

Giada's face grew pensive. "I'm still trying to wrap my brain around the idea myself."

Ceyric drew his brows together. "What?"

Skyler motioned for them to enter the ship. "We can discuss insanity once we're out of Earth's atmosphere."

Giada hesitated at the foot of the ramp. "You expect me to fly halfway across the universe in this?"

"Excuse me." Lady Parsec sounded miffed. "I am quite capable of seeing you through the galaxies –"

Ceyric interrupted Lady Parsec. "Say that again?"

"I am quite capable of seeing you through the galaxies –"

"Not you, Lady."

"Uncanny, huh?" Skyler loved the look of surprise on Ceyric's face.

"You sound just like Lady Parsec." Ceyric eyed Giada.

A voice blasted across the field. "Surrender yourself."

Surrender? Right, like Skyler would consider it with his cargo needing to be several galaxies away in a few days.

"I can't go with them." Giada raced up the ramp.

Skyler cupped his hands over his mouth. "I'll be back. Soon." His WD vibrated. The incoming message was from the commander at the League. He didn't open the communication, but flicked a "Sorry, I'm busy at the moment," message back at him.

"Very well then, we'll do this the hard way." The voice from the Amahrian ship boomed back at him.

A warning blast hit the ground beside Skyler, throwing him off balance. If the Amahrians wanted him dead, they'd have hit him. It would give them more pleasure to see him squirm before issuing their penalty.

Ceyric had already raced into the ship and began take-off sequence. Another blast rocked the ship. "Bring up the shields," Skyler shouted.

"Too late, they hit our front thrusters." Ceyric called back. "Lady, deflect all power to rear thrusters and see what you can do about the shields."

Giada screamed. "Get me off this planet, now!"

Lady responded in her usual calm voice. "Deflecting power to rear thrusters."

Skyler pushed Giada into one of the passenger seats behind his chair and pulled the buckle around her waist. Not that she needed to be strapped in, that was just to keep her from getting in the way.

He flung himself into his captain's chair and took control of the panel. "All right Lady Love, do your thing."

"Anything for you." At least one of the duplicate voices was calm.

The ship lifted and tilted to the side before rumbling over the Amahrian ground craft. Skyler had no idea how the enforcers had managed to sneak up on them. He'd have a word with Ceyric later. Usually, Ceyric kept a better lookout for approaching trouble.

A round of explosions hit the ship, causing it to shudder and bounce. Behind Skyler, Giada's terrified yelling became unintelligible. "What's she saying?" Skyler asked.

"I'd rather not say." Lady gave a calm reply. "It wouldn't translate well."

An Amahrian spacecraft appeared above them.

"Sky, there's an incoming message." Ceyric pointed to the screen.

The commander of the spaceship blinked into view. "You can't keep running from this."

"Who says I'm running?" Skyler ran his hand through his hair, wishing he'd retrieved the fedora. "I have cargo to deliver."

"Do you have a permit to carry?" The commander asked.

"Well, actually, it's a passenger." Skyler pointed at Giada before turning to her. He hoped she'd cooperate.

"Are you being kidnapped?" The commander eyed Skyler's cargo, waiting for her to reply.

"Uh, no." Giada's grip on the edge of her chair said otherwise.

The commander leaned forward so that his face appeared larger in the viewer. "Then why are you in such a hurry to leave in the middle of the night?"

Giada tilted her head up. "My fiancé is impatiently waiting for me. I need to get to him as soon as possible." Skyler hoped the commander didn't see her trembling hands.

The commander squinted. "And you are not being coerced in any fashion?"

"No, sir." Giada's voice shook.

The commander turned back to Skyler. His eyes widened until the whites showed under the irises. "Her fiancé can wait a few more days while we straighten out Princess Islae's accusation."

"I'm sorry, Commander, but I am on a time frame here. If I don't get my passenger to her fiancé, then I can't get the sinas to cover my court costs." Skyler flicked his finger at Ceyric, hoping the kid remembered what that signal meant.

Ceyric's hand hovered over his panel. Good, he knew what to do.

"Captain Rohn, I understand, but this will only take a few days." The commander had gone back to leaning in his chair.

"And if I cannot prove my innocence, then I'll have two problems. My head in a kryler and my cargo – er – passenger will not get to her fiancé." Skyler kept his eyes on the commander, but pointed his finger down just out of camera shot. "So I'm afraid I cannot stay."

The commander rested on the arm of his seat. "You do realize that running will add to your other crime."

"Possibly." Skyler pinched his lips and signaled for Ceyric to cut the communication. He turned the craft so it pointed straight at the mega ship.

"Ready when you are." Ceyric gave Skyler a quick glance.

"Shift all shields to the front," Skyler said.

Giada screamed from the back. "I don't want to die. I just want to get out of here…" The rest turned into unintelligible mumbling.

Glad he couldn't understand her, Skyler kept his eye trained on the advancing ship. A round of laser fire bounced off the front. The fore shields had to hold long enough for him to hit the thruster. Even though the Amahrian's were preparing to fire again, they wouldn't use anything to destroy them. They'd never risk an incident with the League over the death of a passenger.

"This is crazy." Ceyric wiggled his fingers in anticipation. "I don't know what you're doing, but I sure hope it works."

Skyler's hand hovered over the thruster, preparing to propel Lady past the Amahrian ship. "Ever tried to look at a bee on your nose?"

At the last second, Skyler pulled the nose of the ship up and it zoomed over the top of the enforcer's craft. Everything blurred out, except for the shriek from his cargo.

CHAPTER 9

*G*iada slapped her hands over her eyes, waiting to be obliterated. Nothing happened as silence filled the cabin. Had she imagined it, or did the enforcers not even realize she was on the ship? That commander had spoken to her directly. Yet, he never asked for her name, never looked at her with suspicion. Captain Rohn had managed to get her off Earth without being apprehended. He'd kept the criminal focus on himself. Not that he'd done it on purpose, she supposed. Whatever the reason, Giada was grateful.

The computer voice came soft and seductive. "Well done, Captain."

First, Giada spread the fingers of one hand to peek through with her right eye. Surprised at the stars that lay before her, she dropped her hands to her mouth and covered her open lips.

"Did you have any doubt?" Skyler asked.

"Never. You are a remarkable pilot." Lady Parsec reminded Giada of those times she'd heard her own recorded voice. So that was why the captain had been so fascinated when she'd spoken to him.

Nerves made her giggle and mimic the computer. "Well done, Captain. You are a remarkable pilot. Oh, and by the way, the curl over your left eye looks divine. May I swoon at your feet?"

Skyler didn't turn to look at Giada, but cocked his head to the side. "Ceyric? Did you reprogram her responses?"

Ceyric shook his head. "No."

In slow motion, both men turned to Giada. A scowl spread over Skyler's face.

"What?" Giada couldn't help the laughter. She'd made it off Earth, she wouldn't face the horrible penalty and best of all she was free of –

"The curl over my left eye?" Skyler spoke in a clipped, mocking tone.

Giada stifled another round of laughter. "Whatever swabs your deck, Captain." She burst out again and held her sides. She simply could not subdue her giddiness.

Skyler shook his head. "Women," he mumbled.

"I take offense to that." Giada imitated the computer again.

"Not you, my lady."

"No offense taken," Lady Parsec said.

"You just said you were offended."

Ceyric turned in his seat and flashed a smile while giving Giada a thumbs-up.

Skyler glared at Ceyric. "I'll pretend I didn't see that."

She didn't know why she mocked the captain. Fear always seemed to make her say inappropriate things. She could hear Pops' voice in her head. "Is that really what Father Universe would have you do?" Of course not. At least they were off Earth. Tears threaten to spill as the gravity of the last day washed over her. Her fecklessness disappeared. With her head leaned back against the cushion, Giada let out a soft huff of air.

From the front screen the vastness of space lay before her. The rear screens showed Earth shrinking before it winked out altogether. She tried to tell herself she wouldn't miss it at all. Her parents were her only ties to Earth, and they were both gone. She had no one. Giada drew up her legs and wrapped her arms around them, resting her chin on her knees. She could never go back.

Skyler kept his eyes on the fore screen, his body tense under his flight jacket.

"How long will it take to get to Jesighe?" Giada asked.

"Why are you asking me, when –" Skyler stopped midsentence. "Oh, that was you that time." He turned to Giada. "It's going to drive me crazy with the two of you sounding so much alike." His blue eyes burrowed into hers.

"I can't help how I sound." Giada ran her hands through her tangled hair. She wanted to do something with it before it dried in knots. "Ceyric, where did you put my bags?"

He turned to face Giada. "I threw them behind you."

Giada retrieved the essentials case and rummaged through it, hoping Elspeth had packed a hyler. Relieved, she returned to her seat and ran the styling comb through her damp tresses.

Looking up, she caught the captain staring at her like a scientist examining an amniobiotic specimen.

CHAPTER 10

O nce Skyler established warp speed to get them to the star gate, he turned to give his cargo a look. Not that he had any interest in her since she was already spoken for. Just that curiosity demanded for him to turn around to examine her. The wand she used to brush her hair played with the ends, making it shine like silk. The blue light from the pluerial glowing behind her head gave her an angelic halo. The sapphire color fell around her shoulders and for a moment, she reminded Skyler of a painting he'd seen of angels on Lerix. They had captivating smiles and perfect features. He'd been told by the museum guide not to look too long, or he'd be convinced to never leave. If he looked too long at Giada, would he feel the same?

Giada clasped her hands. "It's bad enough that you watched me get dressed; do you have to watch me brush my hair as well?"

"Sorry." Skyler turned back to face the navigation screen tracking their progress toward their first destination, Singi star gate that would propel them to Jesighe.

He wanted to turn and watch Giada again, but decided her chilly demeanor was not worth the look. Skyler pulled up his WD, then laying the hologram in his lap so that Ceyric couldn't see it, he opened the camera application. Pretending to adjust the collar on his jacket, he attached a tiny lens and watched the miniature Giada sitting in his WD on his lap as she ran her hands through her hair, separating it into three strands. With deft fingers, she twisted the locks, forming a long braid down the front of her shirt. Once she tied off the ends, she continued to brush them until they lay in perfect curls.

He wondered if her hair felt as soft and thick as it looked. He'd love to unbraid it, just so he could find out. Giving himself a mental shake, he took a quick glance at Ceyric. Skyler didn't want to get caught staring at their dazzling cargo. His copilot had leaned his head back and closed his eyes. Skyler went back to studying Giada, her clear complexion, her pale blue eyes, her rounded curves, things he'd not taken time to fully appreciate before. It was such a shame she was already spoken for. He might have enjoyed getting to know her better. After this run, he would double his efforts to find a wife of his own.

Suddenly his cargo interrupted his captivated attention. She sounded slightly miffed, like a jealous girlfriend. "Captain, star gate approach in fifteen gyrocriks. Might I suggest you focus on navigation upon entry."

How had Giada known he'd been watching her? Skyler turned around and faced her. "Cut it out. It's not funny."

CHAPTER 11

*B*efore Giada had a chance to tell him it wasn't her, the ship shuddered and slowed. A piece of debris bounced off the nose of the ship and hit one of the cameras leaving a forward screen black.

"Captain, warp deceleration not within safety protocols, and we are off course." His ship's retort should have held more concern.

An alert blared throughout the cabin, and Giada had to cover her ears. This was worse than evacuation drills at precursory school. Another crash against the ship brought more flashing lights.

"Breach in forward shield. System failure in one hour, fifty-two minutes. Warp drive inoperable. Unable to reach star gate," Lady Parsec continued. "Captain, I suggest you pay more attention to your ship than your passenger." Was that jealousy in Lady Parsec's voice?

"Port! Port!" Ceyric shouted. His palm made rapid movements over the control panel.

The ship gave a lurching spin away from the asteroid field. "We're flying half blind here. Lady, can you repair the camera?" Skyler shouted.

"Negative, Captain."

Giada bit her tongue to keep from screaming again. Surely she hadn't made if off the planet and out of danger just to die in space.

Skyler swiveled in his seat to the side cameras. "Get us out of this mess."

"Yes, Captain." Lady Parsec's voice still held an element of indignation. His ship had a jealous streak, although Giada had no idea what the Lady Parsec would be jealous of.

"Where's the nearest oxygen planet?" Ceyric's grip on his armrests did not match the calm in his voice.

"Myrdon has oxygen conducive to human life, but not recommended as the flora and fauna are inhospitable," Lady Parsec replied.

Giada had read an article about that planet from the only survivor. Suffocating in space would be preferable to being eaten by a violent daffodil, and that was just the flora. One of the animal species could keep a man alive while eating the flesh. The man who'd shared the information had listened to his crewmate dying at the jaws of that creature.

"Lady, my love, are there any other options?" Skyler had slumped in his seat and ran his hand through his errant curls.

"An unchartered moon with dense cloud cover suggests the atmosphere is conducive to oxygen-breathing humans. Possible habitation unknown," Lady Parsec answered, the irritation gone from her voice.

"Then we should set a course to there."

"Unadvised."

"Why, might I ask?" Skyler leaned forward checking the instrument panel where lights blinked in rapid succession like the ones on the enforcers' robot guards when set to kill.

"It is not within reach before degradation of the prow, decompression and loss of air."

Giada blinked several times and shook her head. If she'd heard Lady Parsec right, they were all going to die anyway. Her heart raced. Her palms turned sweaty where she clasped the edge of her seat.

Skyler rubbed his fingers along his jaw, pushing the skin up before swiping his hand over his chin. After a long pause, he straightened his shoulders. "Lady, can you navigate us once we run out of air?"

"I'm sorry, Captain, due to the breach in my hull, my navigation system is operating at seventeen percent."

"Captain?" Ceyric questioned. "We should probably just take our chances on Myrdon."

"You've never heard of Myrdon, have you? There's only been one human who made it off alive. Believe me when I tell you that you don't want to be eaten by something you'd put in a salad." Skyler leaned forward and rubbed his face. "I have an idea. Lady, how's the oxygen in the lower cargo hold?"

"Compromise of its perimeter within safety parameters. Oxygen tanks are sufficient until we reach the moon."

Giada had no idea what the captain was planning. Her stomach spun, the tew threatening to make a reappearance.

Skyler stood and strode to her. After unstrapping Giada, he yanked her to her feet and turned to Ceyric. "Take her to the cargo bay and seal the compartment. There should be enough air to get you two within the atmosphere. Lady will have to maneuver a landing once I'm –"

Ceyric stood. "That's suicide."

"Once you've landed, use the emergency radio to signal for help." Skyler bent and pulled a lever, releasing the latch.

"Yes, sir." Ceyric looked from Giada to Skyler.

Giada's stomach twisted. "You don't have to do this for me."

"I'm not." Skyler returned to his seat.

Ceyric took Giada's elbow and led her to the ladder. "He's doing it for me. He made a promise to my mother."

Giada crossed the deck and put her hand on Skyler's shoulder. "You can't sacrifice yourself for Ceyric. He needs you. I need you." She turned his chair until he faced her. "Isn't there some other way?"

Skyler looked up at her. "If there was, we'd be doing it." His expression softened as his gaze fell on Ceyric. "Tell my mother I love her, and I'm sorry about not giving her any grandchildren."

Ceyric crossed the deck. When Skyler stood, the two embraced in a fierce hug. "I...I..." Moisture hung in the younger man's eyes.

"And stop blubbering like that." Skyler released Ceyric and rubbed at his eye as if merely wiping dust away.

Her own eyes filled as she watched the two men. Her heart ached for Pops, for all that might have been in her life. With her hand over her stomach, she tried to still the trembling. Maybe she'd be joining him after all.

"Get going." Skyler's voice was thick as he pushed Ceyric to the cargo hold.

Giada put her foot on the top rung and eased over the edge. The spacious compartment looked as if it had been a long time since the captain had transported anything living. Crates were strapped down along one wall. At least the floor looked relatively swept.

On either side of the cargo ladder, two jump seats sat against the metal walls. Only one of the seats was padded, the other was solid metal.

"Here, buckle up." Ceyric led her to the cushioned one and helped her adjust the straps. "Things are going to get pretty bumpy if the artificial gravity fails." He pulled the harness over her head and fastened the belt low on her hips. "When things get rough, you'll want to put your arms around your head, and as much as possible, curl into a ball. Fold your knees under you and push against the sides of your jump seat with your legs. It's called brace position."

Giada smirked. "Not that it will help anyway, except to make us feel like we're doing something while we're dying, right?" Giada didn't like being strapped down like some kind of cargo.

Ceyric ignored her comment and went to an intercom panel and spoke. "All right, Captain. We're ready."

He hurried back and strapped himself into the bare metal seat.

CHAPTER 12

$\mathcal{W}$ith the side cameras still operational, Skyler gazed out at the vastness of space. He'd never before thought about how he'd die, but deep inside he'd known his final flight would probably end like this. A blast from an enemy ship would have been preferable. He'd have been obliterated in an instant. Not feel a thing. He'd never imagined suffocating, or the air pressure dropping so low that his blood vessels would burst. Now he'd get to experience both firsthand. It would be over just as fast as being obliterated, but the pain would be more intense than anything he'd ever experienced, including the zithar.

"I'll navigate us as far as I am able and you'll have to take over. Direct all energy to the lower shields. When you've landed –" Skyler tried not to envision his craft exploding on impact. Ceyric could still collect the fee when he delivered his cargo – Giada, he meant. Skyler swallowed. There was something about her. Even though she'd been coerced into being a star-bride, she seemed determined. That's the kind of woman he'd wanted to find.

Skyler shook his head and made sure the latch was secured. Maybe his head in a kryler wasn't such a bad option. Better than that, he should have never listened to Islae. His ship would still be intact. "I'll keep manual control until I lose consciousness. At which point you will resume navigation. Set down in the first habitable piece of land you can find, and once you've landed, send an emergency beacon."

"Yes, Captain."

"Oh, one more thing?" Skyler switched between watching the two side screens, and waiting for the breach in the hull.

"Anything."

"Sing me a story."

"Any particular selection you have in mind?"

Skyler cleared his throat. "Lady, sing to me the one about the man who rode his white horse and the dark-skinned men who tried to kill him."

"The Miracle of George Washington."

Skyler rested his head on the back of his seat and rubbed his brow. "Before you start, turn off this raucous noise. It's giving me a headache."

"Yes, Captain." The system alerts halted. In the silence, background music filled the air. After a swell in the intro, Lady Parsec sang, her voice lilting as if she'd performed at the Galleria.

When she finished, the cabin went still, except for the constant blinking on the control panel.

Skyler touched the viewport screen on his left. "That was your most beautiful rendition of all."

"Thank you, Captain."

"Lady?"

"Yes, Captain."

"I guess this is good bye."

"It has been an honor serving with you, Captain." Lady Parsec's voice seemed to take on a sad tone. "I will miss you."

Skyler kept his eyes on the ship's digital timer. The countdown said eighteen minutes. Was it his imagination, or was it already getting hard to breathe? "Lady, is this the correct calculation?"

She didn't answer.

"Lady?"

Again silence prevailed. Skyler would have preferred the alarms going off to his Lady's silence. He ran his hand over the panel. "Lady!" His desperation to have her speak to him, to give him comfort in his last few minutes made him jump to his feet. "Why in Linition did you suddenly go silent?" Skyler mumbled under his breath.

"Hull breach in sixteen minutes. Initiating Anti-pressure electro-magnetic polarity shifter."

"Who said that?" He turned to see if someone else was on board.

"Parsec E39, Beta One," a digitized, computer generated voice said, sounding like something from the early trials of speech replications.

"Beta what?" Skyler scratched his head.

"Parsec E39, Beta One. Emergency anti-pressure electro-magnetic polarity shifter initiated due to shield breach in fifteen-minutes and fifteen seconds."

Skyler scratched his head. "All right Parsec E39, Beta One, explain to me what you are doing in my spacecraft."

"As per specifications at the time of construction all Stardrifter LParsec 071878s have been equipped with an emergency anti-pressure electro-magnetic polarity shifter in the event of a hull breach."

Lady Parsec gave an audible huff. "Someone should have informed me."

"Your system's installation occurred SD42258. Whereas, the standard protocols predate yours by 53053."

"Someone should have initiated communication between both systems." Lady Parsec sounded just a bit piqued as she spoke.

"The emergency anti-pressure electro-magnetic polarity shifter is designed to be hidden until emergency sequencing has been initiated."

"Emergency sequencing never initiated," Lady Parsec interrupted.

"Sequencing initiated after hull breach," Parsec E39 answered.

"Sequencing protocols should be initiated through my coded regulatory system." Lady's voice escalated in both pitch and speed.

Skyler paced. It was like listening to a cat fight between robots – if that was even possible. Skyler rubbed his chin. "Look, Parsec E39, Beta One… can I just call you Beta One."

"You may call me as you desire," Beta One responded.

"So Beta One, because the emergency override has been initiated, what is your role in all this…exactly what do you do?" Skyler slumped back into his chair.

"I am a failsafe that overrides all other systems in the event of an emergency."

"You have overridden me?" Lady expressed her indignation.

Skyler gave an exasperated huff. "All right, so you've taken over my ship. Do you even know what you're doing and where we're going?"

"Your coordinates indicate the Vularian galaxy, a small moon orbiting a charted planet. Base files suggest oxygen adaptable to humans," Beta One answered.

Lady spoke; "I already suggested that since the alternative was –"

"Uninhabitable due to extremes in carnivorous plant and animal life," Beta One interrupted.

"I already said that, didn't I?" Lady sounded frustrated.

Skyler waved his hand. "Lady, be quiet just for a moment. Let me get to the bottom of this, all right?"

"Yes, Captain."

"All right now, Beta One, you have initiated some kind of override –"

"Yes, sir, the emergency anti-pressure electro-magnetic polarity shifter."

Skyler took a deep breath. For the stars' sake, did the manufacturers have to give such a long name for something only used in an emergency? "For time's sake can we just call it the Polarity Shifter or even better, how about PS?"

"Yes, sir."

Skyler had wished he'd read the entire manual. Apparently this one had a few more features than his previous model. "What exactly does the PS do?"

"The PS is designed to take over the ship, bring up emergency failsafes in the event of a hull breach and seal all leaks." Beta One paused. "Such a hull breach has been noted and the PS is now in control."

"Lovely." Skyler gave a huff. "All right, so who's flying this craft, you or me?"

"You are, Captain, I am unable to navigate. My only task is to initiate the emergency anti-pressure electro –"

"I can still maneuver once we are within visual of the moon," Lady interrupted.

"Thanks, Lady, but I'd like to maintain control, and I'd like to live to tell about it." Skyler pressed his hands into his thighs as hope swelled in his chest. Everything was going to be all right after all. He could imagine the look of surprise on Ceyric's face once he'd landed. Right now, he had a ship to fly.

He gave a whoop of relief. "Hey, Beta One, any chance you can repair the cameras?"

"Negative, Captain. Those have been irreparably damaged. Suggesting that you use peripherals to land."

"You can't repair the cameras?" Skyler asked.

"No, sir. The PS only allows the hull to stay intact until we reach sufficient altitude in which oxygen may sustain life."

Skyler clutched the fabric on his pant leg with one hand, while taking control of the panel with his other. "Then we are going to experience a great deal of turbulence."

CHAPTER 13

*G*iada kept a steady watch on Ceyric. If they managed to land without being incinerated, her cargo mate would most likely incur the worst injuries since his harness had him strapped to metal. She had to prepare herself mentally, just as she did every morning before going into the trauma center. "Are there any medical supplies on board?"

Ceyric glanced up at her. "Yes, above deck."

"Good." Giada wiped her sweaty palms against her thighs. "And an extra supply of water?"

"Tanks are below deck."

Giada nodded.

With an eyebrow raised, Ceyric asked. "Why all of sudden are you interested in the ship?"

She'd keep her concerns to herself. It wouldn't do either of them any good to panic. "Just assessing what we have and what we might need."

Ceyric went back to studying his hands. "If we survive."

"So, you and Skyler are related?" Giada tried to make small talk to hush her own fears.

Ceyric turned his hands over and flexed them into fists. "He and my dad are brothers."

"You don't look much alike." She studied his ruddy complexion and light brown hair.

Ceyric shifted in his harness. Giada knew fatigue was getting to him. "Our dads share the same mom. My grandfather on my dad's side died before I was born. Skyler's dad is the only grandfather I've known."

"Where's your dad?" Giada asked.

"He was supposed to make a delivery for the Kilpathians, and we lost communication with his ship. The last thing he said was something about space pirates and having to crash land." Ceyric shrugged. "That was almost fifteen years ago. Mom still plays the message when she thinks I'm not around."

The ship gave a lurch to the side, throwing them both against their harnesses. Ceyric's head slammed into the metal pole.

Ceyric grabbed his head like he'd shown Giada. "I think this is it. Hang on."

With her hands tight around the poles on either side of her jump seat, Giada drew her legs up and jammed her knees against the side. The more she could wedge herself, the less she'd get thrown around. Her mouth went dry and her stomach fluttered with each rocking motion. She prayed she wasn't going to be sick.

Turbulence tossed them back and forth, Ceyric taking more of a beating than she was. A sudden whining, like an old motor whirring out of control amplified in the empty space.

"That's not a good sound." Ceyric placed his feet on the ground.

"What is it?"

"That's the ship passing through the atmosphere."

"Is Skyler –" She couldn't even think of what his body would look like after going through decompression as such a high rate.

Ceyric didn't look at her.

"Oh, Ceyric. I'm sorry…I didn't mean…." She wanted to reach out and console him.

They continued to bump and jar as if the whole ship was coming apart. She prayed they'd make it to the surface with minimal injuries.

Suddenly, the ship dropped. Giada could feel the force of the fall as she strained against the harness holding her in place. "I thought this ship was equipped with artificial gravity." A roll to the side left her hanging upside down.

Ceyric didn't answer.

"Are you all right?" Giada wished she could go to him and check his vitals. He looked like he was about to pass out.

The ship rolled again and Giada could only guess they were right side up.

"I don't want to die." Ceyric's body slammed from side to side even though he'd tucked himself into brace position. A jolt flung Giada to the side followed by another one slamming her into the padded rails. Even her fetal position didn't seem to be helping. She knew her body was sustaining bruises, maybe worse. Afraid to look up to see how Ceyric was managing, she kept her head down. One of them had to get out of this with the ability to care for the injured.

Loud random bumps and bangs filled the cargo area as if the entire ship might fly apart. *Ride it out, Giada. Just relax. Go with the movement of the ship.* A sudden jolt sent her flying up against her restraints followed by a hard downward slam. Her head felt like it would detach from her body at any moment. She clenched her teeth to keep from biting her tongue.

As sudden as the turbulence began, it ended with one more bump and she lurched forward. Then came stillness. The lights inside the cargo bay went out, throwing them in pitch blackness.

"Ceyric?" Giada called out to him.

When he didn't answer, Giada felt for the buckles on her harness. A dim red overhead light came on, casting an eerie glow. She could barely make out Ceyric's form, his head lolled to one side and something about his arm did not look natural. "Please Ceyric. You can't leave me alone in this place. I'll never survive."

CHAPTER 14

*H*is fingers stiff, Skyler eased his hand from the armrest. He released the control panel and flexed the fingers on his other, trying to ease the tension. Without the help of Lady Parsec or Beta One, he'd just managed to fly his craft through thick cloud cover, navigated his way through a dense jungle and bring his ship to a full stop in some kind of flat meadow area.

At least that was the last thing he'd been able to see before his side viewports had gone completely black.

Skyler let out a sigh of relief. "Thanks, Beta One."

"It was your exceptional flying that saved your ship. However, your gratitude is accepted on behalf of the crew who installed emergency protocols and the designers of the emergency anti-pressure electro-magnetic polarity shifter," Beta One replied.

"And to you, Lady Parsec." Skyler touched the screen even though she probably couldn't respond due to the power outage.

When the red emergency lights came on in the cockpit, Lady's voice chimed in strong. "It was all your doing, Captain."

He wasn't going to admit he'd been paying more attention to his cargo than the approaching asteroid field. Skyler shuddered as he thought about his close call.

He rushed to the panel and hit the release on the latch. "Ceyric? Giada?" he called down into the red dimness. He hurried down the ladder, descending into the cargo space.

"You're alive?" Giada touched his back before he took the last step.

Her dainty hand steadying him sent a thrill through him, and he nearly slipped off the bottom rung. "Thanks to the failsafe measures." Maybe he was a little more shaken than he thought.

She threw her arms around his neck and held him tight. "I thought you were dead." Giada buried her face in his neck, the moisture from her tears warm against his skin. Skyler liked the way she felt in his arms. He brought his hand up to the back of her head and held her for a moment. It was nice to be the protector.

Giada stiffened. "Oh, Captain, I'm sorry – I didn't mean…"

Hesitant, Skyler released her. He'd never experienced the warmth of a Has'e. He'd heard about how they could captivate a human's emotions. Swaying slightly at releasing her, he grabbed the ladder.

"Be careful. I don't need two patients."

"Two?" Skyler swallowed. "What's wrong with Ceyric?"

Giada led Skyler to where Ceyric was still strapped to his seat. "His breathing is shallow and he's unconscious. I can't tell in the darkness, but I think he may have a broken arm and probably has a concussion, since he's not responding."

Reluctant, Skyler released Giada's hand and reached for the buckles on Ceyric's harness. Giada grabbed his hand. "Wait. We need to brace him first. Is there any way we can get better light in here?"

"Lady, we need more light – can you fix this?" Skyler pushed past Giada and touched Ceyric's head. His fingers pulled away at the touch of something sticky. Blood. The cargo hold gave a slight spin.

Giada caught his arm. "Perhaps you better sit down. You've just been through quite an ordeal. Surviving a crash like that could make anyone a little dizzy."

Skyler nodded and let her lead him to the jump seat. He would let her think it was just the aftershock of dealing with a crisis situation – not what really made him ill – the sight of blood, even after all the years since Yina's death.

He'd always kept his cool in crisis situations, but blood? Nothing could keep him from getting topsy-turvy at that, and especially when it involved people he loved. He stuffed the memory of his sister as far to the back of his mind as he could.

Giada pressed Skyler into the seat. "It's not uncommon for even strong, grown men to experience shock."

With his head resting against the back cushion, he took a deep breath. "You're right. You don't need two patients, do you?" Skyler tried to joke as the panic rose in his chest. The red glow of the emergency light threatened to engulf him in terror.

Giada patted his knee. "No, we do not. Now tell me how to get more light in here."

Skyler shook his head as if it would rid the memory. "Lady, can you restore light?" He noted that Giada's gaze still rested on him, though in the dim glow he could not read her expression.

Lady chimed in. "System's damage repairable, but if immediate light is needed, I suggest opening the cargo door. Atmosphere conducive for human life. Scanners indicate flora and fauna within manageability for sustaining life. I would suggest a laser for protection."

"Then open the blasted door." Skyler hadn't meant to sound so upset. He wiped Ceyric's blood on his pants before the incoming light allowed him to see the red stain on his fingers.

"Opening cargo door," Lady said as the ramp lowered to the planet floor.

Fresh air filled the bay, bringing with it a fruity fragrance. A slight mist wafted along the floor and spread around their feet. Anxious to leave Ceyric's care to Giada, he stood and hurried toward the ramp. "I'll be outside."

"Before you go –" Skyler didn't let Giada finish her sentence. He had to get away from the smell of the blood before he passed out altogether. He couldn't embarrass himself in front of her.

After many deep breaths, he drew his laser and surveyed the area behind the ship. Lady Parsec had carved a long groove through the dense forest, plowing up everything in the ship's path. If this had happened on Earth, he'd have some pretty heavy penalties to pay.

Trees bearing a variety of fruits spread out all around. He'd have to shinny up their narrow trunks to reach them if they ran out of ready-to-eat meals. He hoped they weren't here long enough to exhaust their supplies. His cargo's fiancé might not be so accommodating if she arrived late.

A sudden thought hit him. What if they never got off this planet? Maybe Adam and Eve were simply shipwrecked and had no other choice but to –. Skyler shook his head. Her healer's abilities when they hugged must be playing with his emotions.

Skyler needed to focus on his duties and assess the damage to his ship. Dismayed at the number of missing cameras in the front and on the starboard side, he'd have to make some readjustments by spacing them around the ship. At least his aft cameras were still intact. Those he could also reposition so that he'd have a clear view from the front. He hoped that once he got his ship repaired, he could take her to the nearest space port and give her a thorough going over.

After he assessed the damage, he ran his hand along Lady's hull. "Again, thank you, Lady. You've never let me –"

Before he could finish, something hit him in the back of the neck. He spun around to see what looked like a dwarf with a dart gun pointed at him. His eyesight blurred, and his head spun.

CHAPTER 15

*G*iada watched the captain's retreat and cursed herself under her breath. Or course she'd been relieved he'd managed to survive, but she should not have flung herself into his arms. What must he think of her when she was engaged? Never mind that Giada hadn't met her intended. She chewed her lower lip. No wonder he'd made a quick exit.

Ceyric gave a low moan.

With the light filtering in through the door, Giada felt Ceyric's pulse. Even though his breathing was irregular, his pulse was strong and steady. Looking at the straps and where they pressed over his chest, the breathing problem might come from either bruised or broken ribs. The bleeding on his head, though it dripped down the side of his face, didn't look life threatening.

"Ceyric?" She pulled one of his eyelids open, careful not to move his head in case of a neck injury.

She needed those medical supplies, a clean environment, and a lot more light in order to tend to Ceyric.

He rolled his head to one side.

"Careful, there. Let's see what else is wrong." She stepped out of her pants and used the legs to tie around his head and around the poles to hold him steady. The pressure would also help stem the blood flow until she could find medical supplies.

"Hold as still as you can. I'll be right back." She gave him a quick pat on the knee before climbing the ladder.

Once on the deck, she asked the computer, "Where are the medical supplies?"

"You will find them in a compartment on the port side of the deck." Her voice sounded flat, emotionless. Maybe Lady Parsec hadn't liked the fact that Skyler had put his arm around her, touched her head.

She didn't want to irritate his computer any further, but she had to find the medical supplies. "And that would be which direction?" Giada asked.

"If you are facing the fore viewport, it is to your left."

"Thank you." Giada looked around the cabin. Fore, meaning before? Or Fore meaning forward. "I'm still confused."

"See the blinking red light over the monitor?"

Lady didn't have to speak to her like she was a four-year-old. "Yes."

"To the left of that light is a compartment. Pull the latch and the door will open."

Along with the medical equipment, Giada found a gray jumpsuit, probably Skyler's. It wouldn't fit her slender form, but she couldn't stand around in her underwear. She should retrieve her bags, but after a quick search she couldn't locate them. The crash must have sent them flying who knew where. Ceyric gave a low moan and Giada opted to wear Skyler's suit instead.

The flight-wear had the same fragrance she'd smelled in Elspeth's AeVe. She breathed in Skyler's musky aroma and ran her hand along the smooth fabric. He'd saved her life again. She would have to make sure she took good care of his nephew as thanks.

Once she gathered the supplies she needed, she hurried back to the cargo hold. Ceyric's eyes were now open and he struggled against the temporary restraint on his head.

She untethered a metal crate against the far wall and used it to sit next to Ceyric. "I'm going to give you a shot of hydropial. That will take away any pain you're feeling so I can splint your arm."

He gave a slight nod.

"How's your neck feel?"

Ceyric shrugged. "Okay, I guess."

"Can you feel this?" Giada pinched the palm on his good arm.

Again, Ceyric nodded. That was a great sign. At least his neck wasn't broken.

"Skyler?" He managed to croak out.

She gave his knee another reassuring pat. "He's fine. I don't know how he did it, but he got us landed, and is out inspecting the ship." She pulled out the jet injector and put a hydropial morphinone cartridge into the port. Then with the end pressed against his pants on his upper thigh, making sure the fabric came in contact with his skin, she pressed the trigger.

Ceyric gave a sigh of relief. "Skyler had no injuries?"

"No, he walked out of here on his own two feet." She wanted to add that other than a quick touch on Ceyric's head, Skyler hadn't given his nephew another passing thought.

Ceyric gave a chuckle and then winced. "His Lady always comes first."

"Yeah, well he was a bit wobbly, too. He might have even been in shock." She didn't want to worry Ceyric with the thought that Skyler might have passed out. Once she got Ceyric stabilized, she'd go check on the captain.

"That medication is going to make you feel a little woozy, so let me brace your arm before I untie your head."

Ceyric reached up with his good hand and felt where Giada had tied the makeshift bandage in place. "I'm supposing there's a reason for all this blood. How bad is it?"

"You have a pretty deep cut, but without a medical facility, it will take a lot longer to heal." Giada wrapped the other leg of the pants around his head.

Ceyric eyed Giada and brought his fingers down to inspect them. "Doesn't feel so bad."

Giada smiled at him. "Head wounds often look worse than they are. You're speaking coherently, you're moving your head just fine, so I think you haven't sustained any brain injuries and have only minimal neck trauma. I'm mostly concerned about this arm."

He winced when Giada touched it. "Ouch. I don't think that shot is working."

"I can give you another."

Ceyric nodded. "Yes, please. I don't want to feel anything."

"That's the plan." Giada gave him another dose. "Now, let's get you into a cleaner environment and someplace with better lighting before I try setting your arm." She looked at the ladder. Even if she could lift him, there was no way he'd be able to climb with only one arm. "Is there some kind of shelter on board?"

Ceyric nodded as if he knew what she was thinking. "In the compartment next to my personal one there's a tent."

"I'll be back," Giada said and climbed back up the ladder.

Once in the cockpit she asked Lady, "Where will I find the tent?"

"The compartments on the starboard side contain all of the necessary survival gear humans require."

She undid the latch and found not only an inflatable tent, but prepackaged food as well. "Lady, would you open the door to the outside so I don't have to keep climbing the ladder?" Giada asked.

The ramp at the side of the ship lowered. Giada placed the supplies on a hover dolly and took everything outside. She breathed in the sweet smelling air and scanned the area.

"Skyler?" Giada called. She left everything close to the cargo ramp and made a circle around the ship. He was nowhere to be found. She clasped her hands under her chin and prayed he was checking to make sure they were safe.

Giada returned to Ceyric who had slouched back into his seat. "I can't find Skyler. What does he usually do when you land in an unfamiliar place?"

"I wouldn't worry too much. He likes to make a quick explore of the area, and set up a safe perimeter." Ceyric managed to stand, but

74

wavered and grabbed the jump-seat bar and slumped back down. "Wow, I must have hit my head harder than I thought."

"Yes, you did. And you're not going anywhere until we get that arm stabilized." Giada went to the medical supplies and located a splint. Once she had his arm immobilized, she secured it around his waist and helped him down the ramp.

Once they reach the muddy dirt, Ceyric turned loose of Giada and sat on the ground next to a massive rock. "That clearing over there looks level. Try that."

Giada used the hover dolly and moved the tent into the area Ceyric suggested. She rolled the cylindrical package onto the ground. Not used to working under such primitive condition, Giada examined the tent. "Are there instructions on how to do this?"

"All you do is just make sure the ground is level, which it is. Pull that lever there, and stand back about twenty feet."

Giada located the knob and pulled. At first nothing happened, so she bent to see if she'd done it right.

"Get back!" Ceyric shouted just as the whole thing inflated and knocked Giada into a puddle.

Ceyric laughed and then winced in pain. "I told you to stand back."

Giada stood, wiped the mud from her hands onto the jumpsuit's pantleg. She strode back to the hover dolly and pulled a pouch of water from it. "So much for cleanliness." She used some of the water to run over her hands and then smeared a sanitizing agent over them. Then to Ceyric she said, "All right, let's get you inside and take care of that arm."

Ceyric eyed her mud splattered clothes. "You might want to change first."

"Ugh. Maybe there's something in one of my bags." She'd have to locate them.

Ceyric gave her a half smile. "Yeah, they might fit you better… unless it was that time he'd got shrunk by a zithar."

"Zithar?"

In his drugged state, Ceyric gave a drunken sounding laugh. "It's an obliterator that can be set to shrink. You should have seen him. He was dwarf size. Oh, but don't ask him about it. It's a rather touchy subject, and he might get short with you." At that he busted up laughing.

Giada chuckled at the thought of Skyler being reduced to half his size. That could be quite a blow to the ego of a man whose only source of flattery came from a sexy computer voice.

Ceyric laid his head back against the rock and closed his eyes, his laughter stopped as quickly as it had started. Giada checked his vitals one more time before heading back into the ship.

CHAPTER 16

Skyler's vision came back in pieces. A dish, barely big enough for a real meal held a green glop that smelled of dirty socks. Next to it sat a mug, also much too small for normal humans. The wooden floor made his back ache, so he sat up crossed legged. He could touch the roof overhead. A distorted face stared at him through the bamboo-looking bars.

Skyler rubbed his eyes, then the back of his neck which burned like it had been set on fire. A welt the size of his thumb stuck out and the offending dart still protruded.

Grabbing the needle, he yanked it out and gave a gasp when it released. "Ah, what in Marada's name is going on here?" he mumbled.

"Jou wake." The dwarfish looking man poked his nose through the bars.

"Yes, I am." He rubbed his neck to ease the fiery pain. Skyler probably shouldn't ask about Ceyric and his cargo until he could surmise what these creatures wanted. No sense in alerting them that there were more.

"Destroy, jou did. Punish jou."

"I had no choice. My ship was losing oxygen and I had to land on the first planet I could find air." Skyler wondered who had taught this creature how to speak English.

"Oxygen? Air?" He squatted on the ground, his nose sliding down the bars as he sat.

"Whatever you call the stuff you breathe." Skyler studied the sticks they'd used for a jail door. He shouldn't have trouble exiting this undersized hut. Yet the closer he approached, the more his neck burned. *Interesting.* If Skyler stayed back, then the pain subsided. He turned to inspect the wall behind him, looking for a chain or rope holding him. He couldn't see anything, yet there was something there that kept him close to the thatched wall. It had to be a kind of invisible tether. No wonder they didn't need a prison cell strong enough to keep a man in.

Skyler scratched his head. "How is it that you speak English?"

"Not first jou destroy."

"Someone else crashed on your planet? Someone like me?"

He nodded. "Jou."

"Me? How could I have crashed before?"

The dwarf gave a huff out his nose, blowing dust around him as he did. "No jou, jou."

"I don't understand."

A man with a deeper voice spoke. "Glit, why are you tormenting the prisoner?"

The dwarf pulled his nose from the bars and scampered off.

A bearded man peered through the bars. "Don't mind him. Diminunites aren't very bright."

"Who are you?" Skyler asked.

The man opened the cell door, stooped and entered. He held out his hand in the familiar gesture of a handshake. "My friends here call me Curse."

"Skyler." Skyler took the man's hand in a firm shake.

"Skyler?" Curse pulled his bushy eyebrows together and rubbed his beard. He shook his head as if to clear his mind of something unpleasant.

"You look a lot like an Earther," Skyler said.

Curse kept his hand at his beard, the stroking stopped. "Earther? Is that what I am? I thought I was a giant, but I didn't speak their language when I woke up in this same cell. Took me a while to communicate with them."

"How did an Earther get here?" Skyler asked.

"Same way you did." He sat crossed legged in front of Skyler. "By Marada's stars, it's good to speak to someone like me. I thought that after I hit my head, I'd just forgotten how to speak their language. Took me a while to realize I wasn't one of them. And that I'd actually flown in on a ship like yours."

"Glit said that I had a death sentence because I crashed into their forest." Skyler clasped his hands in front of him.

"Not as harsh as some of their other punishments." Curse laughed as if he was in on the biggest joke.

"Well, I'm not quite ready to die yet." Skyler rubbed the invisible tether. "How did you manage to gain their trust?"

Again Curse laughed. "That happened after my execution."

CHAPTER 17

With Ceyric resting comfortably, Giada decided she probably ought to try and find Skyler before she set the bone. He might need to hold Ceyric's shoulder.

She followed his tracks in the mud around the ship, but couldn't see where they might have moved off into the jungle. The deep trough around his ship gave way to thick underbrush with fern-like ground-cover springing up everywhere. It would be impossible to figure out which way he might have gone.

A slow drizzle landed on her skin. She pulled the hood of her jacket over her head and hoped the tent came equipped with shower facilities. Once they arrived on Jesighe, she had to look presentable for her fiancé.

Fiancé. As if that was an everyday occurrence for her. She tried to picture the man Elspeth had shown her. He hadn't been particularly tall, but he was handsome enough. With her extremely pale skin set against his darker skin, they'd certainly make a striking couple.

Alem's wealth would leave her wanting for nothing. Elspeth had tried to make Giada understand what taking on the role of a wife to Alem meant. But she'd been so groggy, she found it hard to concentrate. Thinking about it now, she suspected Elspeth had put something in the bath water that made her woozy.

Her thoughts drifted to the captain. She pictured him sitting at his console, his head bowed in his hands – praying perhaps. Or trying to figure out how to get out with his skin still attached. He'd chosen to sacrifice himself for Ceyric. He must really love his family.

Like Giada, he was wanted by the Amahrians. They were both fugitives of Earth. What had he done to merit the enforcers firing on his ship? With a brisk shake of her head, she entered the tent to check on her patient.

Ceyric's brow felt warm to the touch, but not unusually so. She'd love to ask him some questions about the captain. Her patient needed the rest after such trauma. She'd have to ask later.

Giada hoped that once he returned from his exploring expedition, Skyler would tell her the ship needed only quick repairs and would soon be ready to leave this planet and take her to her new husband. Butterflies warred in her stomach. Crashing here had given her time to reconsider her rash decision to marry Alem. Yet, she'd had no choice.

"Father Universe, what have I done?" Trapped here on an unknown planet, with two men she hardly knew, her future husband was waiting for her arrival. What if Skyler couldn't get the ship repaired in time? A man like Alem wouldn't wait long before requesting another bride. Then what would she do? Would she be forced into marrying the captain? Raising children here on a planet they knew nothing about –

"Where did that thought come from?" Giada asked aloud. Just because Skyler was the only man on this planet didn't mean she – "Focus, Giada. We're going to get off this planet." Besides, Skyler wasn't the only man on the planet. Ceyric was here, too.

She checked on Ceyric once more before going in search of Skyler again. Another thorough examination of the ship and surrounding area produced no captain, nor any clues as to where he'd disappeared to.

Giada leaned against the side of the ship. "Skyler, where did you go?" She scanned the huge gouge the ship had carved out of the jungle. It was too bad that their disaster had left such an ugly scar in the beautiful forest. Maybe she could salvage some of the fruit that had smashed to the ground.

Giada looked up into the trees laden with the brightest colored fruit. Some of them looked a little like oranges, others like pink pears.

After searching for a few more minutes, Giada knew she didn't have time until the hydropial wore off and Ceyric would be in extreme pain. She hated to keep dosing him, especially knowing the drug's addictive properties, but she also knew he couldn't stay long in his present condition. She'd have to tackle setting the bone herself, so she headed back to the tent.

Inside, her patient still slept. With a small flashlight, Giada checked his pupils once more and watched the monitor's signal that he was still anesthetized enough for her to do what she needed to do.

Stitching his head wound would certainly be easier than setting his broken arm without a bone amplifier. The portable scanner would have to do the trick.

She placed the scanner over his arm, then watching the screen, she pulled Ceyric's arm until the bones aligned. Satisfied that both the radius and ulna would heal properly, Giada placed the metallic splint around his wrist and forearm, and attached a stabilizer piece at his elbow and connected it to a shoulder harness. Only small adjustments needed to be made for it to fit perfectly until it healed.

An odd noise, like someone breathing hard interrupted her before she could tackle the nasty cut on Ceyric's forehead. She spun around and saw nothing. "Skyler," she called out. "Instead of playing around, you could come in here and help."

Except for the gentle rainfall on the tent above and the monitors on her patient, everything was silent. She checked Ceyric's vitals to make sure he didn't come out of his sleep before she finished attending to his gash. The medical kit contained a cohere and anti-septic wrapped in plastic just like in the primitive hospital she'd worked in in Africa back on Earth. She pulled the handheld swabber from the packaging and ran it over Ceyric's injury. Then with the laser wand, she made sure the under edges of the cut met evenly before she let the heat from the tool seal the subcutaneous tissue, working her way to the outer skin.

The rain had stopped and a chill seeped in through the tent walls. Giada noted the time on her scanner. It had taken her less than one hour to finish patching up Ceyric. The light outside dimmed, signaling nightfall would soon darken the planet. She hoped nothing dangerous would penetrate the tent.

Again, heavy breathing filled the space. "Skyler, is that you?" She wiped her forehead with one of the sterile rags, pulling mud and dirt onto the white fibers.

Just as she looked up, a short man with a blow dart took aim at her. Giada grabbed the metal tray she'd just put all her tools on and flung it in front of her, causing the contents to tumble to the ground. The projectile bounced off the metal with a soft clink and landed in the mess on the ground.

He ducked out the door, and with legs pumping hard, he fled the tent.

With Giada's longer legs, he didn't have a chance to outrun her as he sprinted across the forest floor, cutting over the tracks left by the ship. In the dim light she caught up to him and tackled him to the ground, flinging mud all over both of them. He swung his weapon and hit Giada on the side of the head. She grabbed the end and yanked it from his hands, then rolled him over and straddled his hefty torso, pinning him in the brown slush.

"I don't know what you think you're doing." Giada took the hollow blow gun and broke it in half.

"Destroy, jou," he grunted under Giada's weight, pummeling her with his fists.

"I didn't destroy anything." She grabbed his arms, and with one hand, held both of his, while flinging the weapon out of reach. "Were you going to kill me with that?"

"Not kill, must execute." The little man struggled against Giada's firm hold.

"In my world, those two mean the same thing." The rain had

started again, this time heavier. Giada pushed her hair out of her eyes even as the moisture ran down her nose and dripped onto the creature. She got off him, grabbed him by his cloth-like shirt and dragged him back to the ship.

He kicked and screamed all the way. "Curse. Amel, amel!"

Once she got him into the lower cargo hold, she strapped him into the jump seat, tightening the belts as far as they would go over his shoulders and around his waist. He'd probably be able to struggle out of them with any kind of effort.

"Lady Parsec," Giada called out. "Do you know what happened to Skyler?"

"Negative. Cameras are inoperable."

"Is it normal for Skyler to go exploring without letting anyone know?" Giada continued to keep her eye on the dwarfish man who'd folded his arms over his chest.

"Negative. Consultation with copilot standard procedure."

Giada pulled her eyebrows together. She stared down at her captive. "So what did you do with Skyler?"

"Must execute."

Slumping down on the metal box she'd used earlier, Giada's hands grew cold.

CHAPTER 18

"*E*xplain to me exactly what you mean by execute." Skyler eyed Curse with distrust.

Curse gave a chuckle. "The actual dictionary definition means to complete something with exactness. At least that's what I remember it means. I crash landed like you, although I never could figure out how to fix my ship. That part of my memory must have been lost when I hit my head. I can't remember anything before that day."

"So how did you know they were going to execute you?" Skyler asked.

"Not execute me, but I had to execute a healing of the damage my ship had done." Curse's gaze drifted up to the rafters. "Their chief brought his daughter to me and presented her to me."

"Let me guess, he made you marry her." Skyler was still waiting to get to the explanation of how the whole execution worked.

"No marriage, healing." Again he chuckled.

Skyler had a hard time finding any of this laughable. "Okay, so you had to heal her."

"Not her, the forest." Curse stroked his beard. "She's a healer, not a people healer like a doctor, but a healer of nature. They call her

"Obodoa." Which means as close as I can figure it out, nature's repairer. It's more eloquent when they speak in their own tongue."

"I'm still confused about the whole execution thing."

"They actually blamed that lovely creature for what I'd done." Curse got serious all of a sudden. "Can you imagine that? They said she should have seen me coming and prevented it."

"But it was an accident. Same as me. I didn't mean to cut that gouge in the forest."

Skyler shook his head. "Wait, you said she was lovely? Please tell me their women look different from the men."

"Oh, you mean Glit." He motioned in the direction of the Diminunite who'd had run off. "They are all like that. But once you get to know them and understand their ways, you'll think they're beautiful as well."

Skyler raised his eyebrows. He'd seen a lot of interplanetary species before. And while intelligent life all over the known universe resembled humans in one form or another, these creatures ranked right up there with the Bildens.

"I don't plan to stay long enough to find their beauty. I have some cargo I've got to deliver. So as soon as I can repair my ship, I'm out of here."

"First you have to execute."

"What do you mean?" Skyler didn't have time for this nonsense. He had to get back to Ceyric and make sure his cargo had managed to heal him.

"You have to rebuild what you have destroyed."

Skyler clapped his palms together. "Okay, so I cover the trench and plant a few trees. How hard can that be?"

"I just finished repairing what I'd damaged. In fact, in the exact same spot you just destroyed."

Skyler didn't mean to gape. "How long have you been working on it?"

"I believe I have seen the passing of forty-two seasons. I don't know how that equates to Earth time." He gave another rub of his beard.

"Did you have a beard when you got here?"

Curse shook his head. "No. I tried keeping it short with a knife, but that was just too painful, so I left it."

"Then I'd say your facial hair says you've probably been here ten or twenty years. My cargo's delivery won't wait that long."

"Once you've been here a while, you really don't want to leave anyway. And whatever cargo you're carrying, you can probably use here." Curse gave a half smirk although it was hard to tell under all that hair.

Use here, huh? Skyler closed his eyes and pictured her hair as pale as dust rings around Tyrus, and her skin as smooth as the fur on a wriggle's neck, her lips the color of strawberry azaleas. It wasn't her looks that made her who she was. As a Has'e her healing abilities could be useful in a place like this. But who would she give her heart to here? He eyed Curse for a moment – too old. Ceyric? Too young. Skyler avoided thinking it. Then again, would it be so bad to have Giada's heart? No, that was selfish of him. He had to get her to her fiancé. Skyler had already collected half of his commission for her.

Skyler tried to stand. Both the ceiling and the tether at his neck prevented him from doing so and he slunk back onto his knees. "What is this?" Skyler reached around to where the pain subsided only when he sat down.

"Call it a leash of sorts." Curse rubbed the back of his own neck. "They released me a few days ago after I fixed what I'd destroyed."

Skyler nodded in the direction the Diminunite had scampered off. "He seemed rather frightened of you."

"They are a rather interesting species – frightened one moment and fearless the next." He stroked his beard again. "You wouldn't happen to have a razon in your ship by any chance?"

Skyler knelt forward. "Don't go near my ship."

"Ah, secret cargo, huh? Smuggling?"

Skyler let out a huff of air. "If you must know, I'm delivering a starbride to Jesighe."

Curse raised his eyebrows. "Is she a look?"

"Yes. But don't go near her." Skyler remembered how Giada had looked when he dragged her from the tub. And then when she'd changed in the AeVe – not that he'd actually been able to see anything because it was so dark. He shook his head as if to clear her from his mind.

He couldn't afford to get tangled with another man's cargo. And he certainly didn't want anyone else sweet-talking her away. If he ever wanted to get paid for his delivery, he'd better make sure his cargo made it to her destination.

"Ah, she's that much of a look, eh?" Curse's eye gleamed. Ten or twenty years without looking at an Earth woman, and a beautiful one at that, Skyler knew exactly how Curse would react to someone like Giada.

"So where is this cargo of yours? Did you leave her tied up in your hold?" Curse got up, his back stooped to keep from hitting the ceiling. "Sounds like a damsel needing rescue."

"If you must know, she's a healer and is tending to my copilot." Skyler reached out to stop Curse, the tether burning where it pulled on him.

"I think I'll shave first, and then have a look at your look." He winked before he turned and walked out hunched over.

"Leave her be. She's already engaged," Skyler shouted after him. Curse better not lay a hand on her.

CHAPTER 19

*N*ow that Giada had managed to capture one of the planet's inhabitants she had no idea what to do with him. If she left him to go in search of Skyler, or to check on Ceyric, this little man would escape and let the whole tribe or village, or whatever they called their clan know what she'd done.

She paced around the cargo hold trying to decide what to do. "Did you see a man about this tall?" Giada put her hands at what she figured was around six feet. "Dark curly hair, blue eyes, strong jaw?" She pointed to her own features hoping it translated.

"Curse." The little man said.

"No, his name's Skyler."

"Skyler." He shifted his eyes as if looking for something.

"Did you shoot him with your dart gun?" Giada held her hands up in the shape of the weapon she'd broken and tossed into the forest.

"Shoot jou not." He kicked his feet against the jump seat making the metal click with his soled shoes.

"I know you didn't shoot me." Giada sat on the seat and tried to talk to him as if he was a small child. "Tall man." She held her hands above her. "Hair." She grabbed one of her locks and wrapped it around her finger. "Curly." Pointing to the man's breeches, she continued. "Dark hair, like this." Then she grabbed the man's chin. "Jaw. Strong." She then pointed to her own eyes. "Blue like mine, but darker."

"Skyler."

"Finally. Where is Skyler?"

"Curse."

Giada growled in frustration. "Not Curse. Skyler."

"Skyler. Curse. Jou."

Giada slapped her knees. "Whoever this Curse is he's done a horrible job teaching you how to speak proper English."

"He has, has he?"

Giada jumped at the male voice.

"Curse!" The little man shook his head and tried to wriggle out of his straps.

"Oh, no you don't." Giada shoved him back and turned to the bearded man standing on the cargo ramp. "And who are you?"

"Curse."

"Curse! Curse! Curse! Jou! Curse."

"Hello Glit. It looks like you've gotten yourself tethered. Now you know how it feels." Curse rubbed the back of his neck.

"Where is Skyler?" Giada took a step away from the imposing figure. "His nephew and I have been worried sick about him."

"Ready to –"

"Execute!" Glit interrupted before Curse could finish.

"They're going to kill him? For what?" Giada couldn't believe that this moronic pygmy tribe had taken her captain hostage and intended to execute him for Marada knew what.

"Sit down and I'll explain it to you." He scanned the cargo hold. "You wouldn't happen to have a razon would you? It's been a long time since I've had a good shave."

"They are about to kill Skyler and all you can think about is a shave?"

"Execute just means he has to fix what he broke." Curse eyed the ladder and stood underneath the opening above. "This lead to the razon?" He put his foot on the first rung.

Giada made a grab for his leather breeches as Curse headed up the ladder. "Excuse me. You can't just wally into someone else's ship and take over like some kind of pirate."

Curse reached down, took her chin and eyed her like she was property. "Skyler was right. You are a look." His gaze went the length of her then back to her face. "Nice full lips, too. He didn't mention that."

Giada jerked away. "Excuse me, I have a patient to check on." Giada clench her hands. So, Skyler had called her "a look", had he? Well, he'd certainly had his fill of looking, first in the tub and then in the AeVe. She marched down the ramp toward the tent.

"Hey, Honey," Curse called after her.

She halted as if the name had slapped her off her feet. "Where do you get off calling me *Honey?*" Giada had had enough of being called honey and sweetheart and sugar. Those were endearments saved for people who really cared. The sooner she got off this horrid planet and into the arms of a man who might actually care about her the better.

"Look, I didn't mean anything by it." Curse crossed the cargo bay.

Giada held up her hand. "I don't know what Skyler told you about me. I'm not available, and if I was, I wouldn't be interested. I've had it with men."

Curse smiled under all the hair around his mouth, showing a set of white teeth. "You're going to get married to a complete stranger. I'd say you were interested in men."

"Interested in – Ugh!" Giada didn't finish. She had no reason to explain anything. Besides, it was none of his business why she'd chosen to accept a proposal from a man who lived several galaxies away.

Curse took a tentative step toward Giada. "I'm sorry, we got off on the wrong foot."

She held her space. "All I know is that I want to find Skyler, get him to fix his ship and get the perdition off this planet."

"Execute." The little man had managed to wiggle out of the harness and stood next to Curse.

"Yes, I know." Curse patted his head like he might a dog or small child.

"Besides the ship, what exactly does he have to fix?" Giada asked.

"The trough he dug and repairs to the trees he ploughed down."

That would take years. Giada didn't have time to wait for him to fix it. She had to get to her fiancé, not that she was anxious to marry a stranger, but she certainly didn't want to live in this primitive place. Her time spent on the African continent made her much more appreciative of her civilized comforts. "How long do you suspect that will take?"

"Took me long enough to grow this." Curse stroked his beard. "And my damage wasn't nearly as severe as that done by this craft."

"No." Giada's knees went weak. She'd be too old to have children by then. All of her prime career would be spent working with – she looked at the little man – creatures she knew nothing about.

"Give or take a few days." Curse continued stroking his beard.

Giada left the cargo bay and stood at the bottom of the ramp and eyed the havoc Skyler's ship had caused. If they'd brought accelerant from Earth, then at least the trees could get an early start. But to have to smooth out the still smoking trench he'd carved would take way too long.

Curse stood behind her. "It's a doozy for sure, almost exactly like the one I created."

She turned back to Curse. "So where is Skyler? Why didn't he come back with you and get started?"

"They'll keep him tethered for a few days as part of his punishment, and then the chief's daughter will give him instructions on making reparations." Curse headed back toward the interior. "Now about that razon."

"Is that all you care about?" Giada followed him into the cargo hold.

"Of course not." He put his foot on the bottom rung. "You think I wanted to stay on this perdition forsaken planet when I knew I'd come from somewhere else? You think I like not knowing who I am or where I came from?" Curse advanced on Giada. "I tried radio contact with the outside world, but the atmosphere, while it looks lovely under cloud cover, has a magnetic field around it that doesn't permit anything to penetrate it." He turned his back on her and headed up the ladder.

Giada followed him. "I can't spend the rest of my life here, either. I have a life – or rather I had a life. I don't want any more taken from me than I already have."

"Then I suggest we find a way to get off this planet and get home." He disappeared into the cockpit above. Giada followed him up the ladder.

He touched the panel and Lady Parsec sprung to life. "Good evening, Ceyric." She used the same sultry voice as she did when Skyler greeted his ship.

"Who?" Curse withdrew his hand.

"You don't have the same voice as Ceyric. Please forgive me." Lady Parsec sounded confused. "But you do have the same code signature as Ceyric."

Giada eyed the hairy man with suspicion. "That's impossible." In all her work as a medical practitioner, she'd never seen two people share the same code signature. Those were something that could never be replicated.

A sick feeling started in the pit of her stomach.

CHAPTER 20

Skyler crawled on his hands and knees trying to figure out just how far his tether let him go. Each time he reached the point of pain, he drew a line in the dirt. Less than one meter was as far as the tether allowed him to move without discomfort. He tried standing, but that was worse than moving forward. If he could stretch the limits of the distance, kind of like a ductile band, eventually he'd be able to break free.

Before long, he managed to move in an arc that extended beyond the first set of marks he'd drawn on the ground. Stretching the invisible tether a little more, he ignored the burning at the base of his skull.

Finally, exhausted, he leaned against the back of the hut. Rain water seeped in under the sticks that formed the walls and ran down the outside of his blue flight suit, sending a chill through him.

After resting for a few moments, Skyler tried to move to the outer arc, but the tether held him behind the first set of marks. He gave a growl of frustration. He'd have to start all over again. This time, though, he wouldn't rest between stretching the distance he could get his leash to go.

By the third try, he'd managed to reach the flimsy stick door. He grabbed a hold of it and pulled himself forward, willing his body to ignore the burning pain in his neck. Skyler gritted his teeth, straining to pull the door off its leather hinges. Maybe he'd overestimated just how strong the door was. His muscles tightened as he grasped the bamboo-like sticks. The stalks bent and crackled under his exertion. First one snapped then another. His spine felt the same way, as if any moment it would snap apart and his head would go rolling off his shoulders across the hut back to where he started.

A great pop in his brain sent shots like crackles of electricity through his neck and down his spine, as if someone had shot him with a laser. His eyes burned like bees stung them repeatedly. He waited to black out, signaling the end of his miserable life in this wretched place.

Falling forward, with half his body on the outside of the hut, his legs twitched behind him like they had minds of their own – every conscious moment pure agony. Before long his vision cleared and his body stilled, but the sensation of electricity continued to run their fiery fingers through his veins.

Several unarmed Diminunites screamed and scurried from their positions in front of other hut-like prisons.

The crackles within him gave a final spark and shot out through his extremities. Skyler struggled to his knees just in time to see a girl, a child perhaps, run to him and wrap her arms around his waist.

"Noye, Noye," she cried, her arms squeezing him as if she had the strength to stop him.

Like a man drunken on Honani, he stood, dragging her up with him, her feet dangling in the air. He stumbled, but managed to keep his balance in spite of the extra weight around his waist.

The rain continued to pour down on him. This time it ran into his jump suit.

"Noye, Noye!" The child buried her face in his belly.

As gently as he could, he lifted the child's face to his. "You must let go."

Her deep green eyes with their doleful expression caught him off guard. Her face did not look anywhere close to the adult ones around him. This one had a cherubic charm about her. The rain ran down her face, plastering her bangs to her forehead and pulling her brown braided locks around her cheeks. "Noye – peez – noye."

"I have to get back to my ship."

A Diminunite approached. "Execute." He stopped in front of Skyler and held a dart gun to his lips.

Skyler should have been able to not only pull the miniature child off of him, but knock the weapon from the older one's hands. He fell to his knees, unable to stand any longer. "All right, all right. I'll execute."

The child released her hold, but kept a firm grip on his leg. "Seeyo, Pap. Execute."

The little girl's father answered in some language Skyler couldn't understand. He took the girl's hand and pulled her next to him. With his eyes full of wariness, he asked, "Trust jou?"

Skyler nodded. He didn't know why he felt compelled to keep his word with these creatures. All he'd have to do was fix his ship, sail away and never return to face the punishment they'd exacted on him. The Amahrians had expected recompense from him as well. But he'd run from them. His error here had been an accident. His crime on Earth hadn't been his fault either. Now as he faced this tribe of Diminunites, Skyler knew that once he finished the task of executing, however long that took, he had to return to Earth and fix what he had done.

CHAPTER 21

*G*iada followed Curse onto the flight deck. He rummaged through Ceyric's locker until he found a pair of scissors and a razon. She put her hands on her hips. Really? All he thought about was shaving? She huffed and left the deck to return to Ceyric.

When she entered the tent, Ceyric sat on the edge of the cot, pain written all over his face. "Do you always leave your patients to suffer like this?" he asked.

Still fuming from her encounter with Curse and Glit, Giada grabbed an injector and loaded the cartridge. She tightened the leg of his pants and jammed the flat end against his thigh.

"Ouch." Ceyric rubbed the entry point. "I take it you found Skyler?"

"Not yet. But I did meet two inhabitants of this Marada-forsaken place." She removed the empty cartridge and threw it into a plastic crate set up to hold trash.

"Do they know where Skyler is?" He tried to stand, but leaned to the side and fell back onto the cot, careful not to catch himself with his broken arm.

Giada sat on a stool next to him. "I suggest you stay put for a day or so, at least until the pain is bearable without the aid of hydropial." She touched his shoulder. "I'm sorry about that." She hadn't meant to take out her frustration on the kid.

He shrugged. "Whoever it is you met must have really put the twixit in your suit. So where is Skyler?"

"Apparently there's a tribe of creatures that live here – they look a lot like dwarfs on Earth – anyway, they're holding Skyler for a couple of days until he repairs the mess his ship made when we crash landed."

"That could take a long time." Ceyric laid back on his cot.

Giada rummaged through several crates before finding one with bedding. "Here." She handed him an inflatable pillow. "Get comfortable. It's going to be a long night."

Ceyric jammed the pillow under his head. "Just keep the hydropial coming, and I'll be fine."

"I can only do that for so long before you get addicted. Believe me, you don't want to have to detox here." Giada closed the entrance to the tent and dragged her cot closer to the opening. If anyone tried to get in, they'd have to get through her. If all the rest of them were like Glit, she'd have no trouble taking them out.

"You don't need to sleep there. Just activate the shield." Ceyric said, without looking at her. "This tent model seals as tight as the ship."

She smirked at Ceyric. "And we know how well that went. Although, if a dart gun is all they have, then they shouldn't be able to penetrate the outer skin, right?"

"A laser blast couldn't even get through." Ceyric's speech slurred as he became drowsy with the medication.

"Just to be on the safe side, I'm going to stay right here." Giada pulled extra bedding from the crate and made up her cot in front of the door.

"Oh, one more thing." Ceyric's voice came through mumbled. "Put your hand over the panel and lock it. Oh, one more thing. Change the security identification on the key pad –" That was the last she'd heard from him before soft snores came from his side of the tent.

Since security identification needed a handprint, she'd have to do that in the morning. At least she could lock them in for the night.

Giada settled onto her cot and gazed up through the transparent top. She tried to imagine a cloudless sky above and how different it might look from this spot in the universe. She'd always wondered what it would be like to visit other worlds, to learn how to heal other life forms. If she was going to be stuck in this dreary, rainy place, then perhaps she could see what she could do to help these creatures.

It was too early to go to sleep, yet Giada was simply too tired to stay awake. With the harrowing events of the day, she couldn't keep her eyes open and she drifted to sleep.

A heavy weight pressed down on her, as if someone had dropped an Armorer on her. Whatever it was crushed all the air out of her lungs as she struggled to remove whatever had fallen on top of her.

"What are you doing in front of the door?" Curse rolled over the top of her and landed with a thud on the floor on the other side of her cot.

Giada turned on one of the low output lights. "How did you get in?" Curse had made good on his desire to shave and he wore a clean jumpsuit, probably Skyler's.

"Signature pad." He held up his palm. "Hey, it worked in the ship."

Of course, that's what Ceyric meant; change the signature on the pad so that Giada had control over who came in and out. "Where's Skyler?"

In the dim light, Curse perused the perimeter of the interior. "Oh, he's still in prison...if that's what you want to call it." He stopped at Ceyric. "Who's that?"

"The captain's copilot." Giada wished the man had gone back to his village and left her alone. "When will I get to see Skyler?"

Curse continued to lean over Ceyric. "Tomorrow, maybe. Or the next day. Why? You interested in the captain, because if you're not –"

"I am only interested in the captain because he's supposed to take me to my fiancé." The fact that she'd put her arms around him and hugged him was purely out of gratitude.

"Hm. Me thinks the lady doth protest too much." Curse sent her a raised eyebrow glance before turning back to Ceyric. "So how badly is he hurt? He looks awfully young to be flying a spacecraft."

"He had a very good teacher." Giada let out a huff and lifted the tent flap. "Shouldn't you get back to where ever it was you came from?"

"I will in a bit." He watched the monitor attached to Ceyric for moment. "You never answered my question. How bad is it?"

"Broken arm, wound on the forehead. He'll survive." Giada moved her cot away from the doorway. "Thank you for checking on us. Now that you've seen we're fine, you can leave."

"Just be careful. This may look like a hospitable place, but it can be quite dangerous." Curse stepped out the door and hummed a tune, the melody growing more distant.

So far, the only real danger Giada had seen was a dwarf with a blow gun and Curse, and they were both more annoying than dangerous.

CHAPTER 22

Skyler had known dark before, but never quite so penetrating as this. The fire sticks these primitive creatures used for light barely broke through the night. After he'd promised the chief he'd begin reparations in the morning, Skyler tried to make his way back to the ship to check on Giada – he meant Ceyric. Yes, he had to check on him. He worried that perhaps Ceyric had gotten hit on the head harder than what it first appeared.

He shouldn't worry. He'd left his nephew with a healer. Even a half-blooded Has'e had a gift. He touched his shoulder where she'd held him. Her soothing hands had sent a jolt through him, unlike anything he'd ever experienced. It had to be because of who she was. She was the reason he'd let his guard down so that the Diminunite could sneak up on him.

With the torch held in front of him, Skyler tried to get his bearings. He couldn't be sure which way the village lay in correlation to the ship. Perhaps he should have asked. Night was the worst time to navigate through a dense forest, even if he'd been able to see the stars.

A roar split the air and made the hair on the back of Skyler's neck prickle. Judging by the volume, this creature meant double danger. The last thing Skyler wanted to do was get caught out in the open when whatever he'd heard spotted him. Hopefully it scared easily with a torch. Most animals on Earth retreated at the sight of flames.

A twig snapped and Skyler spun around.

"How did you manage to get away?" Curse held a torch of his own. He looked hollow and gaunt without his hair.

"With much pain and suffering." Skyler rubbed the spot where the invisible tether had been. "For a primitive people, they sure know how to keep their captives, don't they?"

"You have no idea what they are capable of." Curse's voice sounded bitter. He shook his head. "And that roar – it's as bad as it sounds. Keep your torch with you at all times. Oh, and if you raise it over your head, she'll think you're bigger."

"Just how big is this creature?" Skyler brought the torch higher. Now he really wished he had his laser.

"It's not how big they are, it's where they hang out at night." Curse looked up.

From the branches in the trees above him, yellow eyes looked down. Its fur must have been black like the night as it blended in with the foliage. Skyler jumped and nearly dropped his torch. "Marada's lash! She's staring at me."

"I have to get back to the village. The chief's daughter invited me for supper. It's considered incredibly rude not to show up. I wouldn't want to be tethered again." Curse nodded behind him. "Your ship's that way." Curse left Skyler standing under the tree facing whatever that thing was.

These people had odd customs, ones he had no intention of learning. He'd just have to find a way to clean up his mess and get his cargo to Jesighe. His palms grew sweaty as he thought of Giada in another man's arms. That was ridiculous to feel jealous when he hadn't even known her for more than a day.

The creature gave another roar, her ensuing snarl rattled his nerves. With his adrenaline screaming for him to run, he resisted the urge. He knew that most predators like a good hunt, liked to chase their prey.

Skyler went from gripping the torch over his head to swinging it in circles around his body, the light burning arcs in his retinas. The creature jumped through the branches from limb to limb, keeping just over his head. At any time, it might pounce down on him. Skyler had to keep reminding himself not to smell like fear. He'd faced monsters like this before, but never without his laser blaster.

When he got within a few paces of his ship, he noticed a pale blue light coming from the interior of the tent. Good, she'd found the shelter. If he could make it inside, he knew the creature couldn't penetrate the shield protecting it.

The beast dropped down between Skyler and the tent. This thing looked like a morph between a velociraptor with a body built for agility, and a panther with its rounded head. Its black fur shimmered, reflecting the torchlight as if it had been set on fire. The creature raised its head, sniffing the air, never taking its eyes off Skyler. Snarling, it lifted the corners of its snout, showing razor sharp teeth that could have belonged to either species. It rose up on its hind feet and towered over Skyler, releasing a roar that pierced his ears and left them ringing.

Whimpers came from the inside of the tent. "This was supposed to be a habitable planet."

The beast turned at the sound of her voice. Its claws lashed out and raked the side of the canvas. He raced to the tent. When he saw that the creature could not penetrate the tent, he breathed a short-lived sigh of relief. They'd activated the shield.

"Skyler?" Giada called, as her silhouette fell across the canvas wall. Whatever she was wearing did not hide her trembling curves.

Skyler held the torch out while the creature sniffed and clawed at the tent. "You're safe. He can't get through the field."

The creature turned its attention back to Skyler. If it couldn't reach the meal inside, he was a much easier snack.

"Captain?" Her shadow disappeared. "What is that out there?"

Skyler kept the torch swinging above him. Each pass of the flames reflected in the creature's eyes. "That's the sound of a hungry monster; black, fangs, drooling. Looking at me like I'm lunch." He backed away from the tent taking small steps toward his ship. "Whatever you do, don't let the shield down. Do you understand?"

"But Captain, I can help."

"No!" He yelled when her hand went up to the panel. "There's nothing to keep you safe if you drop the shield. You have to protect Ceyric."

The beast gave another roar, its breath made the sparks sputter off the end of the torch. He could make a run for the ship, holler at Lady Parsec to let down the ramp.

His mother had a kitten once that loved to play laser tag. Up the wall and over the furniture that silly thing chased the spot until it would drop, exhausted. Skyler hoped instincts for the same kind of game held true for this species as it did for cats back on Earth.

He flung the torch as hard as he could in the opposite direction of both the tent and his ship. His legs pumped against the wet ground. He took a quick glance behind him. The stupid animal had fallen for it and went after the torch.

His feet slipped under him and he fell into a bog with a splash. The beast turned, its claws trying to grip the ground. It looked like the thing was more stable in the trees than down below.

"Lady! Open the cargo door," Skyler hollered as he regained his footing.

With a whir of hydraulics, the ramp lowered. Skyler scrambled the distance to the hold, the beast roaring behind him. Its jaw snapped in sharp cracks.

Skyler tripped and fell across the metal flooring.

With a chomp on his boot, the beast grabbed his foot and dragged him down the ramp. "Close the ramp!" Skyler screamed.

"Closing ramp." Lady Parsec brought the metal walkway up. the beast slid over the edge, letting loose of his boot in the process.

Skyler rolled away from the entrance and breathed heavy. He lay on his back, listening to the angry roars of the frustrated beast outside.

The pain in his ankle shot up his leg. Afraid to look, he crawled to the ladder and struggled up the rungs using his arms and hopping on his good leg. Agony jolted through him with each jump.

When he reached the cockpit, he rolled onto the metal deck and panted, waiting for the intense pain to ease. This was worse than the invisible tether. It was a good thing he had hydropial on board.

He pulled himself to the medical cabinet only to find it empty.

CHAPTER 23

*E*ven though the shield around the tent would keep the roaring beast outside, Giada still cowered under her cot. Logic told her that whatever could tear its way through the tent would certainly find her there. Fear kept her under the flimsy bed.

She put her hands over her ears. Her body shook as she scrunched her eyes closed.

When Skyler gave the command for his ship to lower the cargo door, she knew that the hold was probably big enough for whatever was trying to catch him. Maybe she'd heard him wrong and he meant the gangplank. She hoped he'd be able to get up fast enough.

Through her hands pressed over her ears, she heard Skyler screaming out in pain. Whichever one he'd chosen, he hadn't been quick enough. Her stomach knotted as she tried not to imagine the beast ripping the captain to shreds. With her hands clasped in front of her, she bowed her head. "Please, Father Universe, let him survive. We'll never get off this planet without his skills."

Ceyric didn't know how to fix the ship, and Curse? He'd crash landed here, too. Had star craft changed enough in the last couple decades that he wouldn't know how to repair it?

Every time she closed her eyes, images of the captain flashed through her mind. Ones she couldn't bear to think about.

A series of thumps filled the air before everything went quiet. The steady fall of rain beat against the tent.

Giada didn't know how long she stayed under her cot praying for Captain Rohn's safety.

Lady Parsec had said that the animal life was safe, or least something they could handle. Whatever had roared had gotten the captain. She dreaded what she would find as soon as daylight came.

If only she'd stayed on Earth and faced her problems, rather than running from them. Her circumstances on Earth wouldn't have left her hiding from something that could eat her.

There were too many *if onlys* and it did no good to dwell on them. That's what her mother had taught her. Just before Mom died, Giada asked her if she would have married Pops if she'd known her heart would give out because she'd married a Has'e.

Mom had stroked Giada's face with her fragile fingers. "Loving your father was the best fifteen years of my life. Raising you was the best ten."

After they celebrated Mom's life, Giada couldn't shake the feeling that her father regretted marrying her, that her death was his fault. Pops had warned Giada. "Guard your heart until you know you have found your match."

"How will you know?" Giada asked.

"You will know. When the right man comes into your life, you will feel it here." He touched her heart. His brows scrunched and his eyes narrowed. "Never mistake infatuation for love. Wait until you are married before you risk your heart. Being only half Has'e, you will enjoy a long life with your husband."

All her life she'd followed her father's advice, except with Lorenzo. She'd almost given him her heart.

Shame hung thick on Giada, remembering how close she'd come. In the same instance, gratitude filled her when she heard her father's words in her mind before it happened. It was the only time since his death she'd felt his presence so powerfully.

Cramped legs drove her from her hiding place. Reason said that if the beast couldn't get in, she'd be as safe on top of her cot as under. She dragged her small bed next to Ceyric's sleeping form. In his drug-induced sleep, his boyish lashes brushed his cheeks – angelic; as if he hadn't a care in the world. Someone so young had a lot to learn about life. Without his uncle, he had no one to guide him. She stroked his cheek with the back of her finger. He didn't budge. His skin was warm, but not feverish.

Tomorrow she'd see if there was an antibiotic in the kit – just as a precautionary measure. Tomorrow she'd make this shelter more livable. Tomorrow she'd tackle the cargo hold and see what else she could find to make their residence on this planet comfortable. Tomorrow – she'd tell Ceyric about his uncle.

When her eyes opened, the light coming through the upper windows cast a soft glow around the room.

Sitting on his cot next to her, Ceyric raised his brows. "Get lonely over there by the door?"

Giada shot up. "Oh, what time is it?" She had no idea how she'd managed to fall asleep.

"Time?" Ceyric looked at his WD. "Depends on where you are."

Rubbing her eyes, Giada's head ached. "How long have you been awake?"

"A couple of hours." He swiped his hand over his digital.

"Why didn't you wake me up? Have you been outside?" Giada flung her legs over the side of the cot, fear knotting in her stomach.

"You slept with your shoes on?" Ceyric's gaze fell on her footwear.

"I, uh, guess I was too tired to take them off." Giada stood and paced. "How's your arm this morning?"

"Hurts here." Ceyric pointed to the splint around his wrist, elbow, and shoulder. "Where's Skyler?"

Giada met his eyes. "I heard him last night, but I couldn't get the door open."

Ceyric gave a huff. "What's wrong with the door?"

"You never gave me access to open it. And Skyler told me not to." She had to tell him why.

"So where is he now?"

That beast could have dragged him anywhere. Pausing, Giada wasn't sure how much Ceyric could handle right now. "He, uh, tried to get in, but there was some kind of creature nearby blocking the entrance. Since I couldn't get the door open, he went somewhere else."

Ceyric shook his head. "He'll probably just sleep in the cockpit."

"Yeah, probably." Or inside the belly of that creature. Giada felt the color drain from her face.

"Hey, are you all right?" Ceyric grabbed her elbow and helped her sit on her cot.

Giada put her hands over her face and rested her elbows on her knees. She dropped one of her clammy hands and ran it over her pants. When Ceyric didn't say anything, Giada continued. "Last night, when I heard Captain Rohn out there, I also heard that thing roar...."

"We've got to find him." Ceyric rushed to the code panel.

She jumped up and ran to him. "Wait."

He knocked her back and left the tent.

Following close behind, she grabbed the splint around his shoulder to stop him. "You don't know if that thing is still out here."

Ceyric winced and pulled away from her. "If you hadn't drugged me last night, I could have been here to help. I could have let him in. I could have fought it off."

"I hardly think in your condition you could have done anything, especially with all the pain you were in." Giada stepped in front of him. "That isn't your fault." She tried to soften his guilt.

"Then whose fault is it?" Skyler limped down the metal ramp from the flight deck, his foot dragging behind him.

CHAPTER 24

"Skyler!" Ceyric raced up the ramp and stopped when he looked down at his uncle's boot. "You're hurt."

"It's probably nothing." Relief washed over Skyler at the sight of his nephew. In his struggle through the night, thinking only of the pain, Skyler had all but forgotten about Ceyric.

Skyler didn't look at his boot for fear he'd see crimson oozing through the synthetic material.

Giada knelt next to Skyler. "We have to get this boot off. But first, let's get you into the tent."

The very thing he'd dreaded was about to happen. He'd look elsewhere – anywhere but at his foot.

Together Ceyric and Giada supported him on either side. He limp-stepped between them. Since he'd stood up, he no longer felt any pain, like his foot had fallen asleep. Once inside the tent, Giada released him and patted the cot. "Lay down here."

She retrieved a pair of scissors from the medical kit. The sharp blade glistened in the light from the transparent windows above.

Skyler sucked in air and wiped the sweat accumulating on his upper lip.

"Let's see what's going on with your foot," she said.

"Shouldn't you give him some hydropial first?" Ceyric asked.

"I want to assess how bad the wound is before I administer anything." Giada placed the edge of the scissors between Skyler's foot and his microfiber sock and cut away both boot and sock. He drew in a deep breath, exhaled and let the room around him spin out of control. He should be in more pain, should feel something in his foot. Maybe that creature had severed it, and that's why he couldn't feel anything.

He tried to swallow, but it stuck in his throat as Giada ran the scissors up his pant leg, stopping below his knee.

"This isn't good." She cut the lower half of the pant off.

"It's black." Ceyric moved in closer.

Skyler raised himself up on his elbows. He knew he shouldn't have looked, especially when he saw that the skin from his ankle to his knee was dark as night. The top of his foot was completely black, except for the blood that seeped out of the puncture wounds across the instep. Dry heaves anchored in his jaw and tore at his stomach.

"Grab him something to throw up in." Giada motioned to the plastic crate used for their trash.

Skyler leaned over the side of the cot, but with an empty stomach all he could do was dry heave.

"Now can you give him some hydropial?" Ceyric touched the top of Skyler's head.

Skyler wiped the sweat from his brow. It wasn't the pain, as he didn't feel any. It was the sight of his leg. Poison. If Giada couldn't stop the spread, he'd die.

"I don't dare give him anything until I can figure out what kind of poison this is. I don't know how the hydropial will react with the venom." Giada touched Skyler's leg. "Can you feel this?" she asked.

Skyler gave a slight shake of his head. "No. Is that bad?"

"Most venomous creatures create symptoms that you're not experiencing, except for the nausea."

And Skyler should probably tell her that being sick to his stomach wasn't from the reaction to the bite, but from the way it looked. "I have a confession."

"You're not going to die." Giada peeled opened a packet with dressing in it and placed it over the bite marks.

Skyler ran a hand through his hair. "It's not that kind of confession. It's, well…I can't stand the sight of blood. It makes me ill."

Giada paused, then looked over at Ceyric's bandaged head. "Well, that would explain why you were in such a hurry to leave the cargo bay yesterday." Giada dabbed at Skyler's wound.

"Can you do something for him?" Ceyric held the crate.

Giada shook her head. "I have to know what kind of poison this is, and then, I don't know. Maybe there's some kind of natural antidote here on the planet."

Curse would know. He'd lived here long enough. "Ceyric, go to the village and find a man named Curse."

"Who?" Ceyric asked.

"I can't explain it right now. Just go." Giada threw the bloody rag into the waste bin.

"Where's the village?"

The room around Skyler spun again, and he laid his head back on the cot. "Please, Ceyric, just hurry and find him. The village isn't far, not more than a few kilometers to the east.

Ceyric grabbed a laser before touching Skyler's shoulder. "I'll show that beast who's the boss."

"Oh, and watch out for the Diminunites with dart guns." Skyler stared up through the windows overhead at the darkening clouds.

"Dart guns?" Ceyric asked. "Against a laser?"

"Don't shoot the little guys; put it on stun when you get to the village. Until then, use it as protection against whatever other wild beasts might be out there. Besides, I don't think you're up to the kind of punishment they'd dish out if you killed a creature that might be sacred to them."

Ceyric ran his hand over the panel. "How will I find Curse?"

"He's the only other human on the planet." Skyler wiped his mouth and leaned back onto the cot.

"Shouldn't be too hard to find then." Ceyric sealed the tent flap on his way out.

Skyler watched Giada for a moment as she examined his leg.

"You really can't feel this?" She poked his foot.

"Feel what?" Skyler held one hand over his stomach and rose up on the elbow of the other. Her fingers pinched his shin. Shocked, he looked at the blackness spreading up past his knee and inching its way toward his thigh.

Giada removed her hands and stepped back.

"You're a Has'e; can't you heal me?" Skyler tried to reach out for her. She moved out of his grasp.

"I...I..." Tears welled up in her eyes. "I killed a man using my gift."

He beckoned for her to come closer. "I'm sure it was an accident."

Her face contorted in fear. "I don't know. He didn't seem that sick and something happened, his heart stopped. I couldn't get a pulse...If I'd taken him to the.... He died. I...I didn't know...." She took another step back. "Maybe because I was only half Has'e."

"Okay, so you're half alien." Skyler didn't care if she had three heads at the moment. "Has'e are great healers."

"We should wait for Curse." Giada didn't meet his eyes but looked back at his leg.

He beckoned her. "At the rate the poison is traveling, I have maybe an hour before it reaches vital organs and then my heart. I'll be dead by the time they get back."

"That's why the enforcers were after me." Giada pressed her hands against her chest. "They knew...."

Skyler leaned as far forward as he could and took her hand, pulling her over to him. "I'm sure you didn't mean for him to die. You're not the kind of person who would deliberately kill someone." He placed her hand over his heart. "If I die, who will repair the ship? Who'll get us off-planet? Ceyric needs me. I made a promise to his mother." Skyler gave her hand a squeeze. "You can do this. I have faith in you."

"I..." Giada's hand tensed in his.

Skyler rubbed the back of her hand with his thumb. "Believe in yourself." He pointed to his leg which had gone completely black beyond the area that Giada had cut his pant leg to. "Please, give it a try. I won't turn you in to the enforcers."

"You can't very well do that if you're dead." She pinched her lips together and withdrew her hand.

"And I certainly wouldn't think of doing so if I live." Skyler continued before her confidence wavered. "It's now or never."

After a moment, Giada squared her shoulders and took a step next to his cot close to his head. "Forgive me for whatever happens?" Her gaze locked with his.

"Of course." Skyler watched her pale eyes fill with doubt. "I promise, you'll get off this planet and into your future husband's arms before he even realizes you're missing." He placed his palm on her face, his thumb stroking her silky skin. The warmth of her breath brushed against his arm. The sensation of longing surprised him. He wanted her, wanted to feel her arms around him again, to taste her lips. Ashamed at his thoughts, he pulled his hand back. He had no right to her.

Giada looked down at his hand for a brief moment. She placed her hand on his shoulder, the warmth of it sending jolts through him. "I have to warn you, sometimes a patient experiences a connection to the healer."

"What do you mean?" he asked.

"A Has'e's heart is powerful. Sometimes humans feel the emotions of the healer and temporarily connects to them." Giada eased him onto the cot. "Lie flat on your back."

Such tiny hands, they didn't look sturdy enough to heal. Skyler lay back, gazing into her eyes. Giada unfastened Skyler's jumpsuit and placed both of her hands palms down over his bare solar plexus. The light touch against his skin sent goose bumps over his body.

Her head lowered so that her chin rested on her hands like she was praying. "Father Universe, as your disciple, I invoke your power to heal this man."

CHAPTER 25

Giada's moved her hands upward to his heart. They grew warm against Skyler's skin. Surprised at how quickly her hands flushed with heat, Giada pulled away.

Skyler caught her before she stepped out of his reach again. "What is it?"

"I…can't." She couldn't be the reason for another death.

"Yes, you can." Skyler's eyes flashed in desperation.

Her heart raced. Surely he could feel it pulsing in her fingertips. If she didn't at least try – she had to try, no matter the outcome. She swallowed and took a tentative step. He put her palms on his chest.

The warmth quickly turned to heat as she closed her eyes. She sensed his energies, flowing within. His heart beat, strong and steady, yearning for…she couldn't quite make out what, but for something deep inside. Her hands moved up to feel the rhythm under his ribs where they met at his sternum.

Giada took a deep, cleansing breath allowing light to fill her body. She repeated the words Pops had taught her. "For the healing to work, you must break down barriers to all emotions, even ones you didn't know existed. You may even feel confused by the release of pent up feelings."

She moved her hands to his solar plexus waiting for his spirit's permission to connect with the energy that would allow her to proceed. His mid-torso, warm and smooth under her palms sent sparks of intimacy through her, like she had entered into his most private energy. Once she'd made that connection she moved her hands up to his heart. The brush of his coarse hair tingled under her palms.

Moving her hands to his lungs, she felt the shallow rise and fall, terror bubbling below the surface. It surprised Giada at how deep his fear ran. It was more than just the sight of blood. Perhaps that's where his anxiety originated.

Careful not to delve too deeply lest she take on his fear and be unable to complete her healing, she moved her hands back to his solar plexus and waited for his breathing to slow. She knew that his fear and his deep love were connected. She wondered who it was he loved so deeply.

Like she'd been taught by her father, she chanted, "Zhiyu womon o wushi jingshen." Once he'd settled into steady breathing and his heart rate slowed, Giada knew he was now in a state for her to work on the poison.

She moved down to the puncture wounds and placed her fingertip into the largest of the three. He should have flinched at her touch. Instead, Skyler's breathing stayed steady. "Father Universe, let your light enter here."

As Giada spoke the prayer of the healing warrior, she visualized light flowing from her fingers. With her eyes shut, she allowed her mind to see his skin turning whole. Before she opened her eyes, she let the complete visual take a solid hold in her mind.

She sent healing waves of energy into his leg. "Foot be whole, let the poison vanish. Let life renew this man's body." Removing her fingers, she looked down at his foot. A faint circle surrounded the dark hole and spread out in a mandala-like pattern, the color of his skin changing from black to tan. She placed her fingertips over the second bite mark and repeated her chant.

Again, when she opened her eyes, another mandala circled the wound. It was different from the first as the poison dissipated from his foot. Relief washed over her as she whispered, "It's working."

On the last puncture mark, Giada touched the tip of her finger to it and repeated the same sequence.

In her mind, sparks of light emanated all around Skyler's foot. Giada opened her eyes again to witness the odd formation of a third intricate pattern. The three marks spread and blended together like ink on a watery surface.

Giada brushed her hand up Skyler's shin, sending the curved lines up his leg, diverting the streams over the blackened skin into a river of tangled tattoos. She grabbed her scissors and cut away at the pant leg revealing where the poison had reached his upper thigh.

Like a dam of drawings, the tangles surrounded his leg, cutting off the path of the poison, the blackness receding back down to his foot as if the mandalas were swallowing them. Giada bowed her head. "Thank you, Father Universe."

As she released her breath of relief, she collapsed onto the crate and dropped her head onto Skyler's chest, her energy spent. His skin was smooth where she rested her cheek and the steady rhythm of his heartbeat did not keep up with her racing pulse.

His hand wrapped around her head and stroked her locks, the connection greater than when she'd begun. Love flowed between them as if they'd always been like this. Basking in the feeling, she took his hand and brought it to her lips. "Don't take me to Jesighe. Let me stay here with you."

CHAPTER 26

*D*aylight filled the tent. Skyler stretched. The last thing he remembered was falling asleep on board the ship. Scared to move his foot, he set his gaze on the ceiling above him. Except for a steady beeping that matched his own heartbeat, the room was quiet.

Skyler didn't want to come out of this extraordinary dream and the best sleep he'd ever had. The first part started as a nightmare. The demon grasped him in its teeth and tried to chew off his foot, the pain beyond imagining. He didn't know how long he lay with the darkness surrounding him.

An angel had touched his chest, reached into his heart and held it safe. He kept his eyes closed, savoring the feel of her, reveling in her hair and skin as pale as the moon over earth. Her eyes were like the sea on Odibja. He thought his heart might burst as it swelled with her love. His foot filled with light where she placed her fingers over the wound. Energy shot up his leg under her gentle pressure, restoring not only his physical body, but his spiritual one as well. He didn't want to wake up, to face whatever reality now enshrouded his pitiful life. He wanted to keep her close to him, near his heart, to feel the love between them. Her head lay on his chest, her cheek exquisite against his bare skin – nothing had ever compared to it, nor had he experienced anything as wondrous.

Skyler raised his hand to her head and stroked her hair, matching the rise and fall of his own breathing.

"Giada." His voice came out in barely a whisper. He reached up to touch her hand. Only the fabric of his jumpsuit lay under his fingers. He must have dreamt it. Yet, it had seemed so real.

Skyler finally had the strength to sit up. The dim light made things hard to see. This wasn't the floor of the cockpit where he'd passed out earlier. Where was he? He brought his legs over the side of the cot. He remembered now – the beast had bitten him and his cargo – Giada, saved him with her healing.

The inside of the tent was empty. "Ceyric?" Skyler whispered. "Giada?" No one answered back.

Mumbled voices came from outside the tent. He eased closer to the door.

"I've never seen anything like it," Curse said.

Ceyric answered. "I've heard of it, but I thought it was just a myth."

"It looks like your *look* has quite a gift. Do you think she'd want to stay on this planet and be a healer?" Curse asked.

"Nah, she's supposed to marry some guy on Jesighe."

Skyler shook his head. He dreamed she didn't want to go to Jesighe, that she was having second thoughts about her upcoming marriage.

"What a shame. If I was younger –" Curse said.

Ceyric chuckled. "Yeah, and if I was older."

"We can *what if* all day, but if we don't get off this planet, the only one eligible is the one she saved," Curse replied. "You saw the way he held her. That's a man in love."

Surprised, Skyler stepped away from the door and returned to the cot. He tried to remember what happened the night before. Skyler ran his hand over his cut pant leg and stared down at the exposed skin. Tattoos of circular patterns encompassed the scars from the bite and wound their way up his leg, tying off in delicate knots around his upper thigh. Curious, he pulled up the other pant leg. His uninjured leg had none of the odd marks. However, the hair on his healed leg looked lighter, like the fuzz on a new peach, while his uninjured leg held the familiar coarse hair.

Giada had done this for him.

She'd told him to think about someone he loved. That had been easy. He had adored his sister, Yina. The songs she sung him, the way she'd stroked his head when he was a boy, cooing away the nightmare. It always ended with the ugly memory of her with blood all around. He'd never seen so much blood.

When Skyler had cried out, Marcus bolted through the door, sweating. "What's wrong, bro?" His brother had stopped short at the sight of their sister lying on the floor. "Go get the healer," he shouted.

Skyler couldn't move, his feet riveted to the floor. All that blood soaking Yina's nightgown and pooling around her in a crimson puddle.

"Go!" Marcus yelled at Skyler. It wasn't until his older brother physically pushed him from the room that Skyler found his feet and raced to the healer's house.

Skyler thought about the days that followed Yina's and the baby's funeral. He'd never get over the horror of it.

The door opened and Ceyric entered. "You're awake. Are you hungry?"

"How long have I been out?"

"According to moon time, about two days."

Skyler jumped to his feet. "Two days?"

Ceyric checked the digital. "In Earth hours, only about a day. Time is different here."

The tent flap swung in and Curse stuck his head inside. "Hey, you're up."

"Kind of surprising after having my foot halfway chewed off." Skyler eyed them both. "So you two have your eye on Giada?"

Ceyric and Curse exchanged glances.

Ceyric shuffled his feet. "Of course not. She's way too old for me."

"I'd say I was too old for her – but well, if you don't go after her, then I will." Curse said.

Maybe Skyler would. Especially since they'd most likely stay here for some time, and even if he did manage to fix the ship, Alem would have found another wife.

"Skyler? Did you hear what I said?" Curse asked.

Skyler shook his head. "I'm sorry, what did you say?"

"Already considering the possibility of Giada as your wife?" Curse burst out laughing.

Something about his laugh sounded familiar. It couldn't be. And yet, the probability that Curse was his brother – "Marcus?"

"No, the name's Curse." He shot a confused look back at Skyler.

"Marcus?" Ceyric repeated. "That's my father's name."

Skyler studied the older man with the crag-lined face and the leather skin. Time and the environment had changed him, but he'd never forget that laugh. "You said you crashed here and can't remember who you are?"

"That's what the Diminunites told me. They showed me the ship." Curse shrugged his shoulders. "I don't remember anything before I woke up tethered in one of their huts."

Skyler stepped to Curse and took him by the shoulders. He studied the man's face, trying to find the older brother he'd lost fifteen years ago.

Ceyric's face brightened and then clouded over. "The chance that this is my father is a billion to one. Both of us crash landing on the same planet?" Ceyric's fists clenched and unclenched. "He doesn't even look like my dad."

If Skyler could take a look at Curse's ship, it would confirm that Curse was Marcus. Skyler dropped his hands. "Where is your ship?"

"The Diminunites dismantled it."

"Why would they do that?" Skyler asked.

Curse shrugged. "It cluttered their precious forest, I guess. Besides, it wouldn't do me any good since, number one, I can't remember how to fly one, and number two, it's pretty damaged."

Skyler rubbed his chin, thinking. "You knew that I had a razon on board. You knew how to use it." Skyler paced. "And – your hand matches the same key code signature as Ceyric's. That is not a coincidence."

Ceyric stared at his hand. "There's still no way he should have been able to use my code signature. Those are unique."

Curse studied his palm for a moment and then held it out for Ceyric to see. "Could this have anything to do with it?" Embedded under his skin a chip lay barely visible, like a faded tattoo.

Skyler gave a whoop. "Marcus! It is you!" He grabbed Ceyric's hand and turned his hand palm up. "You wouldn't remember the Gridenti invasion. During that time, the Amahrian's chipped all the families so that they wouldn't get separated. The two of you have matching chips. That's how you were able to get through the shield."

Skepticism still covered both their faces as they examined their palms.

"You mean this is really my father?" Ceyric took a tentative step toward the older man.

"I never knew I had a son." Curse raised his hands, then dropped them at his side, longing clearly written on his face.

"Mom said you had to be dead because you never came back."

Curse rubbed a hand across his eyes. "I have a family? I mean, I always thought I did, but you're it. I mean, I have a son." His gaze drifted to Skyler. "And a brother."

Skyler embraced his brother. "Rayelen will be so surprised to see you. I can't wait to see the look on her face." He pulled Ceyric into their bear hug.

Curse gave another laugh. "And since I already have a wife, I don't think she would approve of me chasing after Giada."

Skyler's face warmed at the thought of Giada and his pulse quickened. "You're right, I think I will keep her all to myself."

When Skyler looked up, Giada stood in the entrance.

CHAPTER 27

A moment, or forever; Giada couldn't tell how long Skyler's gaze lingered on her face. His comment might have been joking, he also might have meant it. She hoped it was the latter. With so many expressions crossing his face it was hard to tell. Maybe she should just go along with the joke and see where it led.

"Keep me, huh?" She tried to make her words light.

Ceyric and Curse exchanged glances before staring at Skyler as if waiting for his response.

He shifted his foot and looked at the floor of the tent. "I...uh..."

Ceyric lifted the tent flap. "We should go check on the ship, or something." He nudged Curse. "Shall we?"

Curse stood there looking stupidly amused.

"Curse." Ceyric tugged on Curse's elbow.

"Oh, right." Curse started to follow Ceyric out the door, then stopped. "I'm sure you'll want to talk about that sauritzen."

"Sauritzen?" Giada asked.

"The animal that bit Skyler –" Ceyric yanked Curse out the door before he could finish.

Giada tapped her fist against her leg and stared down at the floor, afraid to look into Skyler's eyes. "I don't see how knowing its name helps."

"All I know is that it's poisonous. But then so did you." He had almost closed the space between them.

Her pulse raced and her palms grew sweaty. She did not want to talk about the creature that had nearly killed Skyler. "About last night."

Skyler took one last step toward her. "About that." The smell of his sweat and the heat of his body muddled her senses making it hard to think. He reached out his hand and rested it on her arm before drawing her against him. "What happened to us last night?"

Giada did not resist when he laid his palm on her face. She had to explain to him that what he felt might have been nothing more than the patient-healer connection. His eyes held hers in a steady gaze. She drank in the color of his irises, so deep, like the ocean on a clear day. Her breathing turned shallow. She had to focus.

"That usually happens when a Has'e heals a patient." Her voice grew quiet; like she couldn't get enough air to finish. Each word hard to say, she continued, "It usually passes within a day or so and you'll go back to your normal..."

Before she could finish he lowered his mouth to hers and took her lips in a tender kiss. Giada lost herself in the pressure of the softness of his lips, the scent of pomme on his breath.

As she closed her eyes, her heart raced, and her stomach fluttered. Her arms slid up around his neck, and she yielded to him, gently parting her lips.

After a breathless moment, he drew back. "I don't want to go back to normal." He slid his arms around her back and pressed her body close to his, the firmness of his muscled thighs against hers. His mouth claimed hers again. This time the urgency left her quivering against him.

When he released her, she rested her head against his chest, listening to the racing rhythm of his heartbeat. This was the first step in giving her heart to him, the matched pace, and the slight elevation in temperature of their skin. Giada raised her head and pushed against his chest. "I can't," she whispered.

Embarrassed now at what had passed between them, she rested her gaze on his lips. She wanted him to claim hers again, take her to the brink of where her heart beat in time with his. She'd experienced this with Lorenzo, the tempo of their hearts. However, because of Pops' warnings, she'd always guarded herself so that it never went beyond that. Now she wanted to, even ached for it.

Skyler gave a shudder as he held her hands against his chest. "Can't what?"

In all her healings she'd never felt the connection like she'd had with him the night before. She could have easily alleged that his feelings for her had been a result of the healing process, she'd even tried to warn him about it. What she could not account for was the deep yearning for him as she touched his skin. She'd never experienced it before with a patient, and never like this with Lorenzo.

Skyler stroked her fingers where they rested on his chest. His eyes sought hers as he drew his brows together. "What can't you do?"

"I have to save my heart…for…"

"Alem Balek." Skyler released her and stepped back.

"No, well, yes." Giada hadn't thought about her future husband until Skyler had brought him up.

Before Giada could explain the Has'e bonding, a deafening roar split the air.

CHAPTER 28

Skyler covered the short distance to the spaceship. The cargo hold door lay open and the creature that had nearly severed his foot stood on the plank, its head sniffing the air.

"Ceyric?" Skyler yelled.

The sauritzen turned its glowing yellow eyes on Skyler and let out another roar. Above him, the sky crackled with electricity. He didn't know what kind of thunder storms this planet had, but he sure didn't want to get stuck dealing with that as well.

Curse came to a squenching halt, his boots sliding in the mud, splattering Skyler's bare leg. "Myradon's cross hammer," he cursed.

"Where's Ceyric?" Skyler did not take his eyes off the beast as it made a gradual descent from the ship.

"I left him in the hold to test the system's camera relocation patterns."

"Ceyric." Skyler called again. Fear at what the sauritzen might have already done to his nephew tore up his insides.

A sudden downpour hit the metal ramp, drowning out whatever answer Ceyric might have given.

"They're nocturnal. I wonder what it's doing out in the daytime," Curse said.

The water ran down Skyler's hair and into his eyes making it hard for him to lock eyes with the beast. "Maybe this one wants to finish his kill."

The beast had not taken its eyes off Skyler as its tongue darted in and out of its mouth, its teeth snapping in between. With another roar, it pounded down the plank straight at Skyler. Just as it leapt, Skyler ducked and rolled.

The sauritzen slid in the muddy grass. A quick shake of its fur slung gray slime in all directions as it turned again toward Skyler. Yellow eyes focused on him in recognition as its lips lifted in a snarl.

"Do something!" Skyler yelled at Curse, his ears pounded with the tempo of his heartbeats.

"Looooorie Loo a Loorie," Curse rocked back and forth like one of the Earthers from the middle continent trying to tame a cobra. The sauritzen broke its stare and locked eyes with Curse. "That's a good girl. You don't want to eat my brother."

Giada raced to Skyler and knelt in the mud. Her sudden movement turned the beast's gaze back to Skyler. The snarling increased as it stepped into the bog.

Rearing back with its head raised, the sauritzen roared. A sharp pain of fear rolled down Skyler's back and sunk into the soles of his feet. He didn't have time to ask Giada why she'd been so foolish as to leave the tent. The beast crouched on its haunches, preparing to pounce.

Skyler waited for the exact moment when the sauritzen would launch. Keeping his arm around Giada, he rolled her on top of him, flinging her aside and rolling away just as the beast landed where they'd both been.

The sauritzen chomped down, its nose hitting the ground. It shook its massive head and turned toward Giada, teeth bared. The fear in Skyler's stomach turned to horror as the beast grabbed Giada in its mouth and lifted her off the ground. A scream erupted from her before she went limp.

Desperate, Skyler stumbled to the sauritzen, wrapped his arms around the creature's haunch, and stood on its paw. "Put her down."

Skyler hoped his weight on its leg would be sufficient to distract it enough so it wouldn't bite down on Giada. He had no idea how he was going to heal her if the sauritzen pierced Giada's skin.

The sauritzen lifted its leg and stomped down, trying to shake Skyler free.

Good. At least the beast was thinking about something else at the moment. Skyler held on while the creature thrashed, its paw coming down harder each time. He could only imagine the jarring Giada was taking.

"Wait." Giada's voice came out soft as if the exertion was too much for her. "Let the creature go."

He couldn't lose Giada. Not now. Not after…. "If I do –"

Before he could finish, a guttural howl, like a wolf baying, shot across the meadow. Skyler tried to turn toward the sound, but the pivot of the sauritzen left him squinting in the opposite direction.

The sauritzen dropped Giada. She landed face down in the gray mud.

While the creature turned its attention to the new sound, Skyler grabbed Giada's hand and scrambled to drag her away from the confused beast. Keeping her in front of him, he pushed her away from the sauritzen.

Giada dug her heels into the mud, sliding along. "I have to get back to her. I know what she wants."

"I do, too, and she can't have you." Skyler spun around so that he had to drag her away from the still dazed beast.

Giada pulled away from Skyler. "Trust me. If she'd wanted to harm me, she could have snapped me into pieces." She turned back to where the beast and Curse were in a hypnotic dance.

Skyler reached for her wrist and wrapped his fingers around hers. "I'm sure my brother can handle things from here."

Giada didn't pull away from him. "Brother?" Her eyebrows rose in surprise.

At least he managed to take her attention away from the sauritzen. "I know, impossible. But it's him." Pulling her close to him, he wiped the mud from her cheeks.

"How do you know? I mean, he lost his memory, and it could be anyone –" Giada stopped.

"They both have chips in their hands from the Amahrian relocation program. That's how he got into the tent," Skyler said.

Giada brushed at her cheeks. "Oh, that's wonderful. How's Ceyric taking it?"

Skyler's heart hammered. "Ceyric." He let go of Giada and scrambled up the plank to the cargo hold. Once inside, he gulped, praying he didn't find his nephew torn to pieces. "Ceyric?" His voice came out choked. "Ceyric!" He hollered when he got no response.

After searching the cargo bay, he climbed the ladder to the flight deck. A pair of legs stuck out from under the wide expanse of the main control panel. They were covered in splatters of red – blood.

"Oh, Ceyric." Skyler dropped to his knees and covered his face. He should never have allowed his nephew out of the tent until they'd made sure the perimeter was safe.

Ceyric's legs wiggled and he grunted.

"You're alive!" Skyler touched him on the foot. "I'll go get Giada. She'll heal you." Skyler jumped to his feet.

"What?" Ceyric scooted from under the control panel and pulled a pair of phonotechs from his ears.

"You're alive."

"Why wouldn't I be?"

Skyler slumped into his captain's chair. "The sauritzen. I saw it at the door of the cargo hold. You didn't hear it?"

Ceyric shrugged, then waved the phonotechs. "I guess not."

"But you've got blood all over you."

Ceyric chuckled. "Oh, this; it's actuator powder." He brushed the red dust from his pants, the particles falling to the floor.

"Oh." Skyler pulled one side of his mouth up in an embarrassed smile. "I guess with the beast out there, and not being able to find you, and then Giada got attacked –"

Giada! She was still out there with that thing.

He slid down the cargo ladder and raced across the ramp. Both

Giada and Marcus stood next to the sauritzen, petting it like it was the family cat.

Skyler froze. They both knew how dangerous this animal was. At any second it could turn on them and shred them to pieces. "I think that's enough encounters with the indigenous life forms for now." He motioned for the two to back away from the beast.

Giada pressed her face into the sauritzen's fur. "They are really quite gentle if you know how to communicate with them. She waved her hand for him to join her. "Give her a soft scratch here."

"Uh, no." He'd already had too much contact with the beast. Although Giada's healing had been glorious, he didn't want to have to suffer the agony of the sauritzen's poison again.

"She's harmless." Giada continued to caress the beast. "All you have to do is stroke her right here." She tilted her head and flashed Skyler one of her mesmerizing smiles. "Are you skeered?" She said it as if talking to a child.

He hated to admit it. "Yes."

"The man who laughs in the face of enforcers and pilots us through space at the peril of his life, is afraid of a kitten?" She tilted her head and raised an eyebrow.

Well, when she put it that way. Besides, he couldn't have her think he was completely scared to death. He inched forward and stretched out his hand, keeping his body as far from the beast as possible. With one finger, Skyler gave her a quick scratch under her chin. The sauritzen gave a soft purr. When Skyler dropped his hand, the creature nudged him to continue.

"Okay, little mama. That's enough," Giada said. "So, Curse...or would you rather we call you Marcus?"

"Marcus, for sure." He beamed at Giada.

"Anyway, *Marcus* has been telling me how you figured out you're brothers. Father Universe can do all things, then why not bring a family together?"

Skyler wanted to wrap his arms around this amazing woman. Healer. Lion tamer. Incredible faith.

Marcus winked at Skyler as if to say, "You lucky Heavener."

Giada hadn't stopped stroking the sauritzen. "Just so you know, the reason she attacked you is because your ship is on her nest. She just wants her babies back." She turned to the sauritzen. "Isn't that right? That big, old nasty man landed on your eggs."

Nasty man? Is that how she viewed him after she'd kissed him back – and with such ardent passion? "Well, she'd better just as well eat me since her eggs are probably crushed."

Giada dropped her hand and stepped to Skyler, placing her hand on his chest. "Her eggs are fine. They are in a cave underneath us, but when we landed you blocked her entrance."

Suddenly, her fist grasped the front of his shirt.

"Giada?" He caught her hand and held onto her.

Her eyes rolled back. "Help me." Her knees buckled.

Skyler scooped her into his arms before she collapsed.

CHAPTER 29

Giada's eyes fluttered open, the bright light almost more than she could bear. Skyler sat in a chair beside the cot, his mouth slightly open, his hand draped across her ankle. He still wore the muddy, one-legged jump suit, and his chin sported more stubble than just a few day's growth. She tried to remember how long it had been since they'd landed on this moon. Four days? Maybe five. Those were moon days. In Earth time, it might have only been a day or so. Time lost all relevance, except that she was here with the man who stirred her deeper than any had.

She wanted to touch his face, feel the coarse hair under her fingertips. Lorenzo would never have let his beard grow for more than a day. She preferred Skyler's ruggedness.

Skyler's fingers twitched against her ankle. He must be dreaming. She hated to move, but her body ached as if she'd lain in that position for longer than a human body meant to lay. She slid her foot away and sat up.

Skyler raised his head. "You're awake," he mumbled, his voice thick with sleep.

"How long have I been out?" she asked.

"Longer than me. I thought you were going to die." Skyler massaged her foot.

"Die? Why?"

"That sauritzen bit you in your side, close to your heart." He pointed to where a bandage wrapped around her chest.

"But she was so gentle, well except for when she kept trying to get you off her." She pressed the skin and didn't feel anything.

"She must have punctured you while shaking me around." Skyler slid his chair closer to her head and leaned forward. "Something happened to us while you were out."

"What do you mean?" Giada tried to keep the alarm from her voice.

"I'm not sure, but when you passed out, I brought you here, while Marcus ran to the village for the antidote." He brushed a lock of hair off her face. "It was the oddest thing. It's like you were awake, but you didn't respond to anything or anyone but me.

"What did you do?"

Skyler rubbed his palm along his pant leg. "I put my head over your heart and kept saying, "Don't die, please don't die.""

"And then what happened?" Giada's heart raced and she placed her hand over the bandage on her chest.

"This weird-looking light surrounded your head and kind of flowed like a river around us. I couldn't see anything but you."

Oh, no. It had happened. She'd accidentally given him her heart. But she thought that couldn't happen without her consent, and she'd been incoherent, unable to give consent. "And then what happened?"

"By the time Marcus got back, you'd healed yourself." He took one of Giada's hands and kissed her fingertips.

She liked the feel of his lips on her skin. She brought her other hand up to his face and rubbed her palm along his grizzled chin. "How long have I been out?"

"Earth time – about two days." Skyler traced the back of her hand with his thumb, sending tingles up Giada's arm.

"Two days? That's more than four turns of this planet." She tried to sit and felt like the cot had been yanked out from under her.

Skyler caught her and eased her back against the pillow. "Whoa there. You're still pretty weak."

She gripped the edge of the cot. "What do you mean, I healed myself? Has'e can't do that."

"That's what I thought as well, but you did."

Giada blew out a sigh of relief. Not that she didn't want to bond with Skyler, but she'd made a promise to her father. "Then I didn't give you my heart?"

A lazy smile crept up his face. "I wish you had, then you'd be mine." The smile faded. "And not someone else's."

It always came back to Alem Balek. Giada closed her eyes. Why did Skyler have to keep bringing up her fiancé? They might never get off this planet. "About my future…"

"We have plenty of time to think about that." Skyler stood and rubbed the back of his head. "The sun is shining today, it's quite a sight. Would you like to sit outside while I work on the ship?"

They may not have much time, especially if he got his ship operating. Thoughts of sabotage ran through her mind. Not that she knew how to disable it, outside of physically breaking things.

Skyler set up an insta-lounger outside next to the tent entrance and snuggled her into it.

He was right, the sunlight spread gentle warmth across her face, and the pleasant breeze caressed her skin.

Skyler kissed the top of her head. "I don't think you'll have any trouble with the sauritzen, but if you need me, I'll be close by."

Giada nodded.

He sauntered across the meadow to where the cargo plank was down. Marcus and Ceyric had a hologram of the ship up, examining the schematics, at least that's what it looked like from where Giada sat.

She closed her eyes and leaned her head back against the camp chair, puzzling over how she'd healed herself. Maybe the gift had lain deep inside her all along.

The breeze picked up strands of her loose hair and blew it into her eyes and across her face. She stroked the pale ends, trying to untangle it.

A shadow passed over her, blocking the sunshine, and she was sorry the clouds had come back.

"Pale one…see I say."

Giada cracked one eye open. Glit stood with his bulbous nose inches from hers. Startled, she nearly tipped the lounger over. Surrounding her stood a multitude of the dwarf-like people Marcus had called Diminunites.

"Skyler?" Her weak cry for help blew away on the wind.

One of the littlest ones pushed passed Glit, dragging an older man by the hand. "Noye, noye."

The braided locks and pale green eyes accentuated the tiny Diminunite's pixie features. The smile beaming across her rosy lips held a child-like innocence.

"Noye?" Giada repeated.

The little one giggled and stood on her toes, grabbing Giada's face. "Jou no yeave. Baybee jou make." She pushed a dwarfed man toward Giada.

He licked his cracked lips and stuck his broad nose against Giada's. His breath made her gag. She pulled back and pressed her hand against his chest. "I don't understand your language. I have no idea what you want."

The man touched the top of her head and ran his hand down the locks, stopping at the ends, rubbing them between his fingers. "Baybee we make. Big baybee."

That Giada understood. "Skyler?" She tried to cry out, but it came out hoarse and whispered.

"Skyler execute," Glit said from behind the man.

Giada tried to look over the tops of their heads at where she'd last seen Skyler. They were gone.

"Big baybee." The man took her hand and ran his fingers across her knuckles. "Smooth baybee."

Giada tried to pull away from his touch.

Glit started a chant and soon the entire group chanted. "Baybee, baybee."

Several of the heftier-looking men surrounded the chair and lifted her. They carried her like royalty seated on a throne toward the jungle. Her heart beat in her chest. They honestly didn't think she'd want to mate with that little man.

"Skyler," she tried calling out again. Where had they gone?

In the branches above, the black form of a smaller sauritzen jumped from limb to limb. Its eyes focused on hers.

"You have to help me." She wasn't sure if she was pleading with the creature or Father Universe.

Suddenly the animal jumped down from the branches and landed with a roar, blocking their path.

The Diminunites dropped the chair, dumping Giada once again in the mud. One of them pulled out a dart gun.

"No." Giada pressed the end of the weapon down. She closed her eyes and sent a clear picture of Skyler to the sauritzen. *Find him and bring him here.* The beast gave another roar and ran through the trees.

The Diminunites didn't bother with putting her back in the chair, instead, they dragged her bumping along on the muddy ground until they came to a place where huts stood on short stilts up out of the water.

When they reached a large hut with double doors on it, Glit shot his dart gun at her. It stung the side of her neck like a yellowjacket.

CHAPTER 30

*I*nside the engine compartment, Skyler expanded the screen on the digital. "This is what it's supposed to look like."

Marcus peered at the inner workings of the motor. "I've seen this somewhere before."

Skyler gave his brother a slap on the back. "That's because not only could you fly a ship like this, you were the best mechanic on Earth. See, your memory is starting to come back."

Marcus pulled his gaze from the digital. "Great, I remember a stupid little thing inside of the reactor and you think that's something important."

"That's just it – you remembered that it's called a reactor. Once you start working on Lady Parsec, it will all come back." Skyler watched his brother as he wrinkled his brow, just like he used to when he was puzzling over something.

"And soon you'll remember me and mom." Ceyric's hopeful voice chimed in.

Marcus ruffled Ceyric's hair. "I wish I could remember you."

"It's okay, I don't really remember you, either, except for what Mom told me and the digitals she keeps running all the time."

Skyler watched their exchange, hating to interrupt, but the sooner they got the ship repaired, the sooner Marcus could rejoin his wife. He'd even let the Amahrians capture him so that he couldn't get Giada to her fiancé. What had passed between them the night before had left him no doubt that she was the one. His mother would even approve of her. His heart beat faster at the thought of Giada, of holding her in his arms again. He loved the sensation of their hearts beating as one.

Marcus gave a slight cough. "Hey lover boy, we've got to focus on getting your ship back together."

Skyler was surprised at the heat rising in his cheeks. "Oh, I was, uh…come here, let me show you." Skyler led his brother and nephew to the cargo hold. With the tools he'd retrieved from the mechanic's cubby, he unfastened the engine compartment and slipped down inside the large work space.

Marcus stroked his chin. "You know, I've got one of those."

"You still have your ship here? Where is it?" Skyler asked.

"Well, it's in pieces. Here let me show you."

The three of them crossed the meadow. Skyler looked back. Giada must have gone in to lie back down. He was glad she'd regained enough of her strength to be able to take the chair inside with her. A strange sensation seized his chest. If it hadn't been for her, he'd be dead. Her healing touch was unlike anything he'd ever experienced before. He'd felt her love to the very center of his soul. When he was a kid, he once asked his dad what love was.

His father had patted his back and glanced across the room at his mother. "You'll know it. I can't explain it, but there's a certainty."

This time Skyler knew he'd found the one his father described and was sure she felt it too. He wouldn't need to convince Giada not to go to Jesighe. With a pleasurable sigh, he followed Marcus into the jungle.

After several kilometers, a formation of rocks arched across the floor, their gentle slopes barely visible through the lush grasses and shrubs. An opening tall enough for them to walk through comfortably led downward to a massive cave. A green glow came off the rocks, providing plenty of light. If it had been blue, Skyler would have suspected that pluerial technology had come from this planet.

Marcus eagerly led the way around several bends in the downward path. When they reached a massive cave, the dismantled ship looked as if it had just been brought in, piece by piece and laid out in an organized fashion. Marcus led Skyler to the exact parts they needed to repair the engine.

"How about cameras?" Ceyric asked.

"You're a smart kid. If you had set up the order, where would you have put them?" Marcus asked.

Ceyric ran his gaze down the length of the parts and strode to a cryelon canvas covered pile. "Here?"

"You're good. Apparently, you inherited some of my abilities." Marcus gave a shrug. "I'm assuming."

Ceyric smiled. "Skyler's a good teacher, too."

Skyler loved watching the interaction between father and son. It was good to be back together as a family. "All right, let's get the parts we need."

Using a hover dolly, they loaded the items. Before they'd put on the last camera, a deep, rumbling, roar filled the cavern, bouncing off the walls.

The hair on the back of Skyler's neck stood on end and his foot tingled. "You didn't store all this stuff in a sauritzen's cave, did you?"

Ceyric's gaze darted around the cave. "Where's it coming from?"

"Sauritzens do lay their eggs in caverns, but I thought this one was empty – that's what the Diminunites said." Marcus's voice sounded hesitant.

Skyler pulled his laser from its holster. "Just in case."

Marcus nodded.

Guiding the hover dolly, Skyler kept checking down darkened passages that shot off the main tunnel. When they reached the opening, a sauritzen paced, its eyes glowing yellow against the cave light. This one was smaller than the one Giada had tamed. It stopped when it spotted the men and gave another low growl.

Instead of pouncing, it rolled over on the rocky floor and purred, then stood and shook its fur.

It must be a young one that did not understand that humans were a threat.

"What do we do?" Skyler hated to kill it, especially when it didn't seem to be threatening them. But then he also didn't like the idea of another enormous bite.

"I've never seen one behave like that." Marcus kept his grip on the hover dolly.

In many species, loud noises often frightened ferocious animals away. He took the end of his laser and banged on one of the metal pieces they'd retrieved.

The sauritzen jumped to the side and back again, then rocked from paw to paw.

Marcus pulled his brows together. "I didn't know they could do that."

"Shoo! Shoo!" Ceyric had picked up a couple of rocks and banged them together.

The sauritzen growled and turned a menacing eye on Ceyric.

Marcus put his hand on Ceyric's shoulder. "Yeah, you should probably not do that."

Ceyric dropped the rocks. The creature roared and left the cave.

Marcus scratched his head. "That was odd."

"Let's just get these parts back to the ship." Skyler laid the laser on top of the items and pushed the cart out of the cave.

When they neared the ship, the sauritzen dropped from the trees and paced again, repeated the drop and roll, then stood and pranced.

Ceyric eyed the creature. "It's like he's doing a dance."

The beast let out another roar and pounced straight at Skyler. Before he had a chance to grab his laser, the sauritzen pinned him to the ground.

Skyler couldn't tell if he couldn't breathe because he'd had the wind knocked out of him, or because the creature's paw landed square on his chest. It purred, then ran his tongue up his face leaving slime on his chin, cheek and forehead. He didn't dare move for fear the beast would bite his head off with his massive fangs.

"I've never seen them do that before." Marcus had stepped a few yards out of the beast's reach with Ceyric close behind him.

Marcus moved toward the dolly. The sauritzen growled, jumped off Skyler and picked up the laser in its mouth. One sharp crunch and its teeth destroyed the laser.

It returned to Skyler and sat on his haunches, its tapered tail wagged back and forth. Skyler didn't dare move, or even breathe. "Marcus? What do I do?"

He didn't answer.

Skyler's panic rose in his chest and his breathing went shallow. "Well?"

"Uh, you could try scooting back, really slowly." Ceyric did not sound confident.

The sauritzen huffed in Skyler's face and moved off into the jungle.

Skyler sighed in relief and eased onto his side.

"I wouldn't get up just yet." Marcus gestured to the beast as it pounced back, landing on top of Skyler again.

Skyler covered his head. "Please tell me the males aren't venomous."

"More so."

Great. Just what Skyler needed. With Giada's energy spent, he doubted she'd be able to heal him again. Skyler tried to think of something that might be in his ship that would at least distract the sauritzen. Before he could put more thought into it, the beast rolled him over with one of its paws and gave Skyler's face another lick.

Marcus had moved farther away. "It doesn't seem to want to hurt you."

"What does it want?" Skyler stared up into its yellow eyes.

Before Marcus could answer, the sauritzen rolled Skyler onto his stomach. He grabbed the back of Skyler's flight suit in his sharp teeth and tried dragging Skyler, but without success. The beast let go and walked a circle around Skyler before nudging him forward.

"I think he wants you to go that way." Marcus said, hesitation in his voice.

"Thank you, General Obvious. You think he's leading me to his den to eat me?" Skyler stumbled forward as the beast kept pushing him.

"No, they don't do that, they kill first and then drag," Marcus said following behind him. "And he's acting way too friendly for that."

"What do you think he wants?" Skyler tripped forward as the sauritzen kept pushing him.

"I have no idea, but I think I better follow you." Marcus joined Skyler. Over his shoulder, he called to Ceyric. "Take the parts back to the ship. And see if you can bring Giada here so we can figure out what it wants."

Ceyric turned and raced toward the ship.

Once they crossed the meadow, the sauritzen leapt in front of Skyler and paced a couple of times. Then he bounded off through the woods.

"That way?" Skyler wiped the sweat from his forehead.

Marcus rubbed his chin. "Hmm, he's leading us to the village."

Skyler grunted in frustration. He had too many things he needed to get done before he started his reparations of the forest. "At this rate, I'll be an old man before I get my ship fixed."

"I don't think you have any other choice. Unless you want to make the sauritzen angry." Marcus pointed at the pathway leading to the main entrance of the village.

Great. Just great. The sauritzen had led him back into enemy territory. This was the last place he wanted to be.

The beast sniffed the air, cocking his head as if looking for something. Then, crouching low, it took a tentative step onto the cobblestone path, whining as if in pain. His roar filled the air and he flopped to his back.

Skyler knelt and put his hand on the beast's head. "What's going on?" This beast acted as though it might die at any second. Skyler gazed into its yellow eyes. "What's wrong?"

"Well, that's the funny thing about their village. It's like there's some kind of force-field around it that keeps out the vermin." Marcus lifted his shoulders.

The sauritzen's tongue lolled from its mouth and he eased his head against Skyler's leg.

Skyler gave the beast a pat on its head. "I'm not a healer. I don't know what to do."

Struggling to stand, the sauritzen's knees trembled. It was like the rocks were sending shocks through its body. It lifted a paw and put it on Skyler's knee, and then the other until he sat on his raptor-like haunches. It's body still shook as if electricity ran through it. Finally, the beast eased its way onto Skyler's lap.

"Do you want me to carry you?" Skyler asked.

"Oh." Marcus took a step back. "They never like to be held."

"What am I supposed to do?"

The sauritzen nuzzled its head against Skyler's chest.

Grunting under the animal's weight, Skyler stood up and held the beast off the ground. The trembling stopped.

The sauritzen nodded its huge head toward the center of the village.

"Well, let's find out what you want." Skyler turned back to Marcus, who'd kept his distance. "Maybe someone has stolen its eggs or family, or something."

Marcus shook his head. "Diminunites don't eat anything from them. They are poisonous, you know."

Shuddering, Skyler didn't need to be reminded of what their venom was capable of doing.

Once they stepped off the stone walkway, the sauritzen struggled to be put down. With no more visible pain, they walked down the street. The cobblestone path had turned into smooth glass-like stones, only these had the same greenish glow to them as the cave. They passed a woman, out sweeping her porch. She screamed, dropping her broom as she ran back into her home.

Marcus watched the woman's door. "Yeah, that's probably quite a shock to see."

When Skyler stopped to look back at the hut where the woman had fled, the beast stopped, too, and then gave him another shove.

Several men walked around a corner and froze when they saw

them. The older of the men chanted something indistinguishable and then was joined by the two others with him.

"Hello." Skyler gave a little wave.

The men fell to the ground as if bowing to Skyler.

Skyler scratched his chin. "What is going on?"

"Jou Goud." The older one said.

"Goud? I don't understand."

Marcus leaned in close. "They think you're a god."

"I'm not a god." Skyler would never presume to be deity.

"Shh – don't give it away. They think you're a god because you brought a sauritzen through their defenses." Marcus turned to the group and said something in their language before turning back to Skyler.

The men jumped up and motioned for Skyler to follow. As they turned a corner, the sauritzen roared. The Diminunites froze and huddled next to each other.

The beast gave Skyler another shove in the opposite direction.

Skyler gave a quick shrug and headed the way the beast wanted him to go. "We're on important business."

"Jada."

Skyler turned back around. "What did you just say?"

"Zhe dat way." He pointed the way the sauritzen had pushed Skyler.

"Giada is here?" Skyler asked.

As if the name meant something to him, the sauritzen nudged Skyler hard, sending him almost sprawling headlong onto the path.

They were moving further into the center of the village, the huts growing larger and more ornate. The sauritzen stopped in front of a house painted in a vibrant green and trimmed in a darker shade of the same color. Pawing at the double door, the sauritzen roared.

Skyler pushed the door open. The Diminunites behind him all spoke at once, but he couldn't understand them.

Marcus put his hand on Skyler's shoulder. "Uh, this is their governor's home."

"I don't care whose house it is." Skyler ignored the men behind him and ducked through the door and entered a spacious room, at least by dwarf standards. A Diminunite hurried down the hall and came to a stumbling halt when he saw Skyler and the sauritzen.

"Where's Giada?" Skyler stared down at the little man.

The sauritzen had pushed its way around Skyler and growled at the governor. That's who the man must be judging by his attire.

The Diminunite leader hurried out the front door and plowed into the men still standing on the steps.

The sauritzen sniffed and moved down the hall. Skyler followed behind him.

"Giada?" Skyler called.

"Here." Her voice came out weak.

Skyler yanked the door off its hinges. She lay on a bed, with a green coverlet over her. He sat on the side of it and took her head in his lap, stroking her hair. "How did you get here?"

The sauritzen pushed his way around Skyler and settled on the ground next to Giada, his sleek body pressed against the bed.

Giada reached over to the beast and laid a shaky hand on the beast's paw. "Thank you, friend."

CHAPTER 31

*S*kyler had come for her. Giada could only imagine what it must have been like for him to confront the sauritzen. With one hand on the animal, she reached up and touched Skyler's face. The stubble of growth prickled her fingers.

Skyler wrapped his hand over hers and brought her palm to his lips and kissed it.

Giada closed her eyes, savoring the feel of his warmth. Even though his heart wasn't close enough to hear, she still felt the beating of it. Pops had described the connection he had with her mother and how the Has'e knew when the right person came along. With Skyler, she knew.

"I had no idea you'd been captured." He bent and placed several kisses on her brow. "Why didn't you go back in the tent when we left?"

"I didn't know you had gone until the Diminunites surrounded me." She swallowed, thinking about the creepy man who'd licked her face. "I think they want me to marry their leader."

"I won't let that happen." Skyler stroked the back of her hand, sending tingles up her arm.

"How?" Giada released the sauritzen's paw and placed her hand over her heart as if to still its racing.

"I'll tell them we are already married." He kissed her fingertip, then laid them on his chest. "I've given you my heart."

Before Giada could process his declaration, the sauritzen let out a deafening roar as a large group of men stood in the doorway.

The dwarf who had licked her stood in front of the group. "Peez. We reeleez jou."

Marcus's head appeared over the top of the group. "Since they think you are a god, they want to appease you by releasing Giada. But there's not enough room in here. You'll have to step outside."

Skyler gave Giada's hair one final stroke and gently laid her head on the bed. She didn't want him to leave her. Yet, she certainly had no desire to stay here. "Stay close."

"Of course." Then as Giada had shown him, he scratched underneath the creature's chin. Giada noted the confident way he handled the sauritzen.

"Took me years. That's why they never considered me a god." Marcus left the hut.

Crawling on his knees and one arm, Skyler led the beast from the room. The Diminunites spread out in a large circle for them to exit, fear clearly etched on their faces.

Glit entered the room with a stick that looked like it had been cut from the same wood as the door. He pointed the end against Giada's neck. The burning sensation immediately vanished.

Freed from her tether, she rolled onto her side. She'd never felt so weak before. After Herrick had died, she'd still had her physical energy. All she wanted was to get as far from these people as possible.

"Skyler," she called out.

The minute Glit left, Skyler returned to the room and sat beside her, then gently lifted her in his lap. So weak. She couldn't even wrap her arms around his neck for support.

Once outside, he stood and her head rested against his chest, the familiar beating loud in her ear.

Marcus squatted in the path with the Diminunites gathered around him. "Yes, not only is he a god, but you have angered him."

"God?" Giada looked up into Skyler's eyes. "Tell them we are children of Father Universe – who is the one God."

Even these dwarf-like people were His sons and daughters as well. She wished she could remember something her pops had told her, something about every planet having sentient beings. Although they may look different, they all had the same form. Arms, legs, eyes, ears, a brain that reasoned and a heart that felt.

Marcus turned to the group and spoke, but she couldn't understand his words. All she cared about was the protection of Skyler's arms around her as he carried her from the village.

CHAPTER 32

Skyler watched Giada sleep. He couldn't take his eyes off her or pull his heart away from her. He wanted to stay like this forever, to be connected in a way he didn't even understand.

Marcus stepped through the opening of the tent. "How is she?"

Skyler shook his head. "She's really weak. Where's Ceyric?"

"He came after us. He's showing them how to tame the sauritzen." Marcus looked down at Giada. "You know that the only species that can heal like that are the Has'e."

"Yeah, I know." He reached out to touch her hand, looking for the extra ridge that ran along the soft tissue between her thumb and forefinger.

Marcus took a seat near the food crate, opened it and rummaged through the contents. "You know that Earthers are discouraged from bonding with Has'e. They aren't compatible with humans. Our kind die earlier after the bonding – it takes too great of a toll on our hearts."

Skyler continued to stroke her palm ridge. "It doesn't matter to me."

"You've already bonded, haven't you?" Marcus asked.

"No, from what I understand, she has to be conscious for her to bond." Skyler looked back into her peaceful face, her lashes forming crescents against her fair skin.

With a sad shake of his head, Marcus went back to rummaging. "That's good. You'd only get about ten years, maybe twenty with her at best. If you want to stay alive, I suggest you deliver her to her fiancé and forget about her."

Skyler didn't want anyone else. He'd rather die in ten years than to ever consider leaving her. "How do you know all this? I thought you'd lost your memory."

"I don't know. Things have come back to me, small things. I just wish I could remember my wife." The corners of Marcus's mouth turned down, then lifted in a smirk as he tore open one of the meal packets. "I hope her cooking is better than this."

Skyler laughed. "You *have* been gone a long time. Your wife never cooked anything."

A puzzled expression crossed Curse's face. "How so?"

"On Earth, we have replicators."

"Oh." Marcus pulled a fork from the container and ate the meal cold. "After I'm done eating, you want to finish the repairs on the ship so we can move it off the sauritzen's den?"

His concern for Giada had pushed all other thoughts out of Skyler's mind. He didn't want to leave her side, but he also needed to get everyone off this planet. "Will you keep an eye on her while you eat, and I'll get started?"

"Sure." Marcus shoveled in another mouthful. "I told Ceyric not to stay too long since we need to get things moving. When he gets back, I'll leave Giada under his care since he can't do much with his broken arm."

Skyler found the parts they'd retrieved from the cave where Ceyric had left them earlier. Once he lowered the cargo door, he pushed the parts into the hold. First, he'd have to get the cameras working.

"Good afternoon, Lady." It had seemed like a long time since he'd talked to her.

"Hello, Captain. It's good to see you again. Are you doing well?"

"I am, indeed." Skyler smiled, his heart swelling at the thought of Giada.

CHAPTER 33

*G*iada stretched, working out the kinks in her muscles. She had no idea how long she'd been asleep. The sky overhead, though cloudy, had a brightness to it, as though the sun shined through. This planet amazed her for its tropical, beautiful, and graceful wildlife. The sauritzens she'd won over were magnificent creatures. She'd heard a few varieties of birds, at least she thought that's what they were since she hadn't seen any. Their melodies filled the air from time to time. If she didn't want to get off this planet and get to her fiancé, she'd love to stay and explore the beauties with Skyler.

As if she'd been slapped, Giada bolted upright. "Skyler." She whispered his name.

"Oh, he's out repairing the ship." Ceyric sat at a table, working with the parts of what looked like a camera, while an image of a completed one hovered in front of him on his digital.

Giada stood, testing her legs for strength. Not dizzy or light-headed, she still sank back on the cot. She couldn't go to Jesighe and marry a stranger. She wanted to give her heart to Skyler. She'd have to let Elspeth know right away in order to give her time to find another bride. Humming, Giada jumped up. She couldn't help the little dance step come over her as she wallied around the tent.

Ceyric stared at her, his mouth open. "You've made a great recovery."

Giada wanted to shout, "I'm in love!" That didn't even express what she felt. She'd found her bond. "I'm feeling exuberant."

"How about, 'I'm crazy.'" Ceyric laughed.

Giada danced to Ceyric, took his hand and pulled him from his seat, the pieces scattered all over the floor.

"Let's just say I'm happy to be getting off this planet." And for the first time since her mother's death, her heart seemed to burst with joy.

"Ah, look what you did." Ceyric pulled away from her and knelt on the ground to retrieve the parts.

"I'd stay and help you, but I have to find Skyler. We're getting off this planet soon, and I'm going to my man." She gave her hand a swipe over the exit pad and gave a quick wave to Ceyric.

She practically ran across the meadow to the ship. Marcus sat on the rear cargo plank tinkering with who knew what. "Where's Skyler?"

"Cockpit." Marcus motioned over his shoulder.

Giada pressed her hand over her stomach to still the butterflies before climbing the upper ramp.

Skyler's voice came to her like a jeeron on a precooper. "Elspeth, I already told you, we crashed. There was nothing I could do. The magnetic waves around the planet prevented any kind of communication until I fixed the anti-talsmanic."

Elspeth's voice came through crackly, like someone was sawing her voice into pieces. "It's not often we can get a wealthy customer and one with such particular tastes. Do you know how hard it was to find someone with such pale skin and light hair, and blue eyes to match his specifications? You have no idea the trouble Lorenzo and I went through to procure this bride."

Procure? What had Elspeth meant by that? Giada pressed her back against the partition so the cameras wouldn't pick her up. She'd only met Elspeth that once, but the way she spoke, it sounded like she'd known about Giada for a lot longer.

"I realize that," Skyler said.

"He specifically wanted a Has'e," Elspeth said.

"Of course, I understand. You told me all this before." Skyler's seat gave a slight creak. He must have leaned forward.

Giada pulled her eyebrows together as a sickening weight settled over her.

Elspeth went on. "Do you even understand how difficult it is to select just the right girls for my grooms? This one almost slipped away."

Skyler's voice sounded tired. "And you thought that conjuring up a wife for Lorenzo would be enough to make a woman like Giada leave?"

"Lorenzo discovered she can be quite determined. Even after their split, she'd decided to stay on Earth. She's that committed to her work." Elspeth's voice came through a bit clearer. He must have been adjusting the signal strength.

"Yes, I know. And that's why Lorenzo had to stage Herrick's death," Skyler said.

"Do you know it's even harder to find a Kib than a Has'e?" Elspeth asked.

Giada put her hand over her mouth. Herrick was a Kib? An alien who could stop his own heart and go into hibernation? The lump in her throat settled into her stomach. Lorenzo's friend hadn't died after all! That explained why the commander who'd communicated with Skyler had no interest in her. The enforcers weren't after her at all. And the worst part of it – Skyler knew about the whole set up.

Elspeth's voice took on a waspish tone. "You had one job in this plan, and that was to deliver her to Alem Balek. You know what will happen if she isn't there by tomorrow. Do you understand what this will cost both of us? I've already given you half – the half I took out of my own pocket."

"Yes, and I get the other half of it on delivery," Skyler answered, his voice dry and flat.

Giada's breathing turned shallow as she clutched her hands over her chest, her heart ached as if someone had reached in and ripped it out. Her legs went weak and she slid to the floor.

"Then see to it that you get her off that planet tonight. Mr. Balek will be expecting you by star-date 092092."

With her fist in her mouth Giada kept the agonized cry from escaping her.

"Yes, Elspeth." The crackling stopped. Skyler must have closed the communication.

The cockpit sat quiet for so long, Giada wondered if she'd imagined the entire thing. Then soft clicks and ticks filled the room as Skyler went back to work on whatever he was fixing. Cargo meant money. That's all he'd ever viewed her as. Why had she been so foolish as to think he was in love with her? She was nothing more than a pastime.

Without alerting Skyler, she crept back down the ramp. The sky overhead darkened as the clouds thickened. Rain fell, gently at first, and then poured. Marcus had vacated his spot; he'd probably gone inside the tent to help Ceyric with the camera.

Giada shivered as the water dripped on her head and ran down her face, soaking her skin where it penetrated her blouse. She ran into the woods and huddled under a tree. Her tears fell as fast as the water pouring from the sky.

CHAPTER 34

Skyler stared at the blank screen. The money he'd make off his cargo didn't matter anymore. He'd found the woman he wanted to marry, the one he wanted to take home and introduce to the rest of his family. And now that he'd found Marcus, he no longer needed to take care of his brother's wife. All he wanted was Giada. He ran his hand over the captain's chair. "We've seen a lot of good times, huh?"

"Indeed, Captain." Lady Parsec's voice sounded light, like Giada's.

He smiled, thinking about the woman he'd finally found. His heart would never belong to anyone else.

Marcus came up through the ladder. "I finished setting all but the one camera. Ceyric's just about finished with the last one and we can take off right away."

"Great." Skyler looked at his older brother. This planet had changed him, made him age faster. Marcus looked old enough to be his father. "There has never been a day that Rayelen hasn't spoken of you. Her parents always thought she should have remarried."

Marcus's face grew wistful. "Tell me about her."

Skyler would love to see the look on Rayelen's face when Marcus reunited with her. "We'll have plenty of time to talk once we get away from here."

"Where are you planning to drop off your cargo?" Marcus asked.

"She's not cargo." Giada was right; he never should have called her that.

"What are you going to do about her?" Marcus eyed his younger brother.

"I don't know, but I can't take her to Alem Balek." Skyler gave a frustrated sigh. "Let's get the tent down and get this ship off that sauritzen's den, shall we?"

Together Marcus and Skyler crossed the field and entered the tent.

"Giada?" Skyler searched the area for her.

Ceyric leaned over the camera and without looking up said, "She went to go find you."

Skyler scratched his head. "You're sure?"

"Well, yeah. She skipped out of here. Said something about finally getting to her man. I guess she's as anxious to get away as the rest of us." Ceyric held the camera out to Skyler. "All finished."

Her man? Skyler turned to Marcus.

Marcus shrugged. "I told you it would be better for you not to fall for her. It looks like she's anxious to get to Jesighe and to her fiancé after all."

Ceyric stood and arched his back. "You really have fallen –"

"She never made it to the ship." Skyler cut him off. He didn't need these two telling him how to run his love life. Giada loved him. At least, he thought she did. His heart pounded.

Ceyric folded up the work table and laid it in the middle of the floor. "She's probably out collecting some of that fruit."

"She shouldn't be out alone in the forest." Skyler paced in the cramped area. "You never know what else is lurking out there."

Ceyric initiated the disassembly sequence of the tent. "Ah, she can fend off whatever is out there. I've never seen anyone with a gift like hers."

"That was just with one beast." Skyler's stomach tightened, not just at the thought of what else she might encounter. "Hurry up and get the tent down," he said and then raced out the door. They had to get off this planet before anything else happened to Giada.

When he reached the meadow, he gazed around trying to figure out which way she'd gone. The rain had eased up a bit, and a thick fog had settled in its place.

His heart filled with relief as Giada practically floated toward him, her blond hair framing her face like an angel. She carried several pieces of the strange native fruit in one hand, and the female sauritzen was nuzzling against the other one.

"Hello, Captain Rohn," she said dryly.

"Giada." He tried to take her hand, but the sauritzen hissed and stepped between them.

Skyler retreated. "You should have told someone where you were going. As we've both discovered, this planet isn't safe."

Giada stopped. "You're taking the tent down? We're leaving soon, then?"

"Ceyric finished with the camera and I had him retract the tent." Skyler couldn't figure out what had changed.

"I won't feel safe until I'm on Jesighe, in the arms of my fiancé." She lifted her chin.

Skyler eyed the beast for a moment, remembering how Giada had healed him from the sauritzen's bite. How he'd stroked her face when she'd been too weak to move. How he'd kissed her forehead. How he'd carried her, her cheek so close to his heart. Now that she had her strength back, she no longer felt the same. She'd warned him about the connection during the healing process. Was what he felt now a lingering result of that? He looked down at his feet and back into Giada's eyes, hoping to see something there. Her pale eyes had turned cold, that same look she'd given him when he'd dragged her into the night. "As soon as I get the last camera mounted, then, yes, we'll be on our way."

"Let's not stand here talking, then. You have *cargo* to deliver." With that she strode past him, the Sauritzen in tow.

CHAPTER 35

Giada stroked the sauritzen's fur one last time before she marched up the ramp to the hold.

"You don't need to sit down there." Skyler hurried up the ramp after her.

She huffed. "*Cargo* belongs in the hold."

He stomped up the ladder, and without a word, threw her bags down to her.

As Giada sat in her jump seat in the viewer-less compartment, she wished she'd not been so stubborn. Yet she didn't know how she would be able to spend hours staring at the back of his head and keep from crying. She would never let another man see her cry.

She had been so foolish. "Pops, you were right. And I'm glad I listened." She vowed to keep her heart safe until she married. She would be a good wife to Alem Balek. Maybe in time she could love him enough to give her heart to him.

Maybe.

Giada hung her head and let grief wash over her as the tears flowed down her cheeks.

When there was nothing left, she ran the back of her hand over her eyes. She couldn't arrive with blotchy skin, stringy hair, and mud soaked clothes. She'd show Skyler what a *look* looks like.

Giada scooted the larger of the two bags in front of her and flipped the lever. The entire thing unfolded displaying an array of exquisite clothing. A blouse of silk and lace lay on top. A pair of white slacks underneath. Piece by piece she examined the clothing that had all been selected to set off the pale skin and eyes of – her. Her heart grew heavy in her chest. She'd hoped it had all been a horrible mistake. No, this had all been planned…just for her.

When she reached the bottom of the bag, she examined a floor-length gown. The shimmering outer layer floated weightless in her hands. She pulled it up to her chin. She'd never owned anything so beautiful. When she stood, the inner skirt sparkled with hundreds of pluerial lights, filling the hold with blue speckles.

She stared into the mirror on the cover of the suitcase. The color matched her eyes and accentuated her fair skin, drawing out the pink in her lips.

Giada slumped back into her seat. Afraid to look at the exquisite clothing any longer, she stared down at her filthy blouse.

"We'll be entering the atmosphere in a few minutes. I suggest you secure yourself." Skyler's voice over the speaker made her jump.

Giada closed her eyes, trying to remember what Alem Balek's face looked like. Her heart pounded in her ears. It was Skyler's face she saw – his deep blue eyes, his dark curly hair, the way he pressed his lips together when he was concentrating. The way his heart had beat under her fingers.

Again, the tears trickled down her cheek. She couldn't let Skyler see her crying. What would he think? It wasn't like she mattered to him. His plan was to dump her off and head straight to Earth to reunite his family.

"Pops, I've really messed up my life." Giada forced the tears to stop as she wiped the moisture from her cheeks. "I'll be the best wife I can, even if I can never give my heart to Alem Balek."

She wished she could just once hear her father's voice. The cargo hold was still and lonely. "I know you're probably not very happy with me right now. I inherited your strength, so I'll be okay."

The ship gave a bump, signaling they'd entered the atmosphere of Jesighe. Alem Balek was waiting for her.

CHAPTER 36

"Ah, come on, Skyler. You can't be serious." Ceyric swiped his hand over the landing sequence on the digital. "Why do you have to keep jumping off planets before I get a chance to explore? And I hear there's no more beautiful planet than Jesighe."

Skyler didn't answer until they had set down on the landing pad. "I already told you, we're not staying. I'm just dropping off my cargo, and then we're heading back to Earth. You'll have plenty of time to be with your parents there. I'm turning myself over to the Amahrians."

Marcus cleared his throat from the seat behind Skyler. "You're sure this is what you want to do?"

"It is." Skyler ran a hand through his hair. Alem Balek would make Giada happy. He had more money than Skyler could make in twelve life-times. She would never want for anything. Jesighe was paradise with its metropolitan city circled by lush tropical forests, the temperate climate brought in by soft ocean breezes. The snow-capped mountain peaks were close enough for aerial skiing. He gave a slight huff. No wonder Ceyric wanted to stay and explore. Well, he could come back and do that with his parents.

Skyler had no intention of keeping his share of the fee. The cargo delivery money would keep Marcus's family comfortable for years, and they'd have time to travel wherever they wanted.

As he strode down the ramp, he spotted Alem Balek, his dark skin glistening in the sunlight. He must have been sitting in his AeVe for quite a while. The handsome man stood and exited the topless vehicle, his gaze studying the ship, waiting, Skyler was sure, for Giada to walk down the ramp behind him.

"Where is she?" Alem Balek slapped his fist against his pleated pant leg.

Skyler didn't say anything, but ran his hand over the control panel next to the cargo hold.

"You kept my bride in that?" Alem Balek sounded more than disgusted. "What kind of a trader are you?"

"Trader? You talk about Giada as if she was your property."

"Come now, we both know that women have been bought and sold for centuries." He smirked at Skyler.

Skyler swallowed and the lump stuck in his heart and refused to move. He couldn't argue with Alem because that is exactly what Skyler had done. "I have your bride in my cargo hold because that is where she chose to be."

The ramp lowered. The angel stepping into the sunlight stole Skyler's breath. The rays of daylight fell across her shimmering gown, accentuating her pale blue eyes. Her hair gleamed almost white where the sun kissed the curls on top of her head. Her milky skin glowed as if she'd never seen a speck of the mud that had covered her.

Giada's smile molded the lump in his heart into a dagger that pierced his soul. She hesitated at the top of the ramp.

"What a tumble we shall have tonight." Alem Balek poked Skyler in the ribs with his elbow.

Skyler clenched his jaw. "In the contract, Elspeth gave strict instructions that there is to be a waiting period of –"

Alem Balek rubbed his hands together. "I've paid my part and Elspeth is not here to dictate how I treat my *wife*."

"She is not your wife –"

"Yet."

Skyler narrowed his eyes.

"I have the magistrate already waiting." Alem's smile gleamed white against his dark lips, lips he would use to –

Alem Balek held out his hand, beckoning her.

Giada floated down the ramp. Skyler searched her eyes for any signs she did not want to do this. As she passed him, he yearned to feel the beating of her heart matching his own rhythm. "Giada," he whispered.

Her eyes met his. For a brief moment, he thought he saw fear. Giada turned from him and lifted her chin, keeping her focus on Alem Balek. Did Skyler hear a slight intake of air as she passed by him?

Sickened at the thought of Giada in anyone else's arms, Skyler clenched his fists and forced himself to introduce her. "Alem Balek, may I present, Giada Hallspring."

Alem Balek licked his lips like a hungry dog and slid his arm around her waist. "I shall double whatever Elspeth is paying you."

"Keep it." Skyler stormed back up the ramp, passing Marcus as he exited the ship.

CHAPTER 37

*G*iada stood next to Alem in the magistrate's office. Her fiancé scanned the digital for them to sign, making it official before saying their vows. And then what? Giada's stomach had landed in the soles of her feet and refused to budge. The man next to her had a kindly face, but his eyes said he would not be patient with her. How long would he wait? A week, a day, an hour?

She closed her eyes and tried to reach out to his heart, hoping to find goodness there. She felt nothing.

Alem's fingers flipped through the legal images. With a flourish, he placed his hand at the bottom of the document and left his print.

"You sign here." The magistrate pointed to the scanner.

Trembling, Giada held her hand over the place for her to leave her print, signaling she would be Mrs. Balek. She hesitated.

Alem Balek put his arm around her waist. "I know how hard this is."

He did not know. He couldn't know that she loved someone else. Even though Skyler had betrayed her, she would always love him. Giada looked up into Alem's eyes. "You will give me time before...we...?"

"Of course." His grip on her tightened. "But not too long."

She took her lower lip between her teeth. *Pops, please be here for me. I need your strength.*

Giada had never felt so alone and so empty, like the whole universe had abandoned her. She pulled her hand away and stepped out of Alem's arm. "I'm sorry. Give me a moment."

"Anything for you." His words did not hold any warmth, only impatience. Maybe he was as nervous as she was.

She left his side and stepped out into the atrium where the light filtered through the trees. How different they looked with the sunshine behind them instead of the constant clouds overhead. She missed the rain dripping through the leaves, leaving the ground soft, the air quiet.

Giada bowed her head. "Please just let my heart stop hurting." She clutched her hands at her chest. "Father Universe, do you hear my pleas?" Did anyone in the universe listen to her? Suddenly a still, small voice whispered within her. "Be still; be at peace. All is well."

Taking comfort in Father Universe's words, Giada took a deep breath and went back to the magistrate's chamber. "I am ready."

"I've waited a long time for this." Alem Balek stood beside her, but did not put his arm around her.

Giada touched the scanner with her hand. "Thank you Father Universe for my trials."

The magistrate motioned to the door on his right. "Shall we?" A plaque on the paneling read *Chapel.*

Alem held out his hand and smiled at her.

She placed her hand lightly in his, and together they followed behind the magistrate.

The room had a skylight, and the interior of his chambers had a soft glow of sunshine. The rich wood of the pews beckoned participants to share in joyous occasions. "Isn't there anyone here with you? No witnesses?" Giada asked.

"My chauffeur is there." Alem nodded to the short man standing in the back of the room. "He will serve."

The magistrate held out his wrist digital and opened the marriage vows. "Alem, if you will stand here." He pointed to a spot on the carpet. "And Miss Hallspring you may join him here."

Alem and Giada took their places. She looked up at him briefly, then turned her gaze to the green carpet with an inlay of floral patterns in all shades of colors. The green reminded her of the moon where she'd spent the past several days.

"Uh hem." Alem cleared his throat.

When Giada looked up, he held his hand out for her to take.

Before she placed her fingertips in his palm, someone yelled. "Stop!"

Her heart leapt and she dropped her hand.

"Skyler?" It couldn't be. She had watched his ship lift off. Her eyes darted back and forth from Alem to Skyler. Part of her wanted to fly into Skyler's arms. Giada chewed her lower lip. The other part – he'd called her cargo. "What, didn't you get paid enough for me?"

"Giada!" He raced to her. "I have to explain –"

"Explain what? That Elspeth had already sold me? All Lorenzo had to do was set me up." Giada paced. When Alem made a grab for her hand, she jerked it away, then turned back to Skyler. "And when that wasn't enough, he staged Herrick's death so I'd believe him when he said the enforcers were after me. Does that about cover it?"

Skyler slumped, defeated onto the pew and stared at his hands. "Yes. But you still can't marry him."

"And why not?" Giada clenched her fists letting anger take hold, the hurt too much to bear. "I'm all bought and paid for."

"Because I gave you my heart." He lifted his head and met her eyes.

Giada pulled her eyebrows together. "What do you mean?" Only Has'e could give their hearts.

Skyler held her gaze. "When I got back on my ship, I called my mother. I told her everything that had happened. The blue light, the healing, the way our hearts beat together. I never knew I had Has'e blood. It comes through my great-grandmother." Then quietly, so only she could hear, he whispered. "I love you, and that's why I gave you my heart."

Alem closed his fists and held them in front of him. "Just because you gave her your heart does not obligate her in any way. That was your own foolishness." He grabbed Giada's hand and turned back to the magistrate. "Mehlo, have this man removed, immediately."

The magistrate rushed out the door and returned as quickly with several men. They grasped Skyler on either side.

Alem continued, "You have no rights here. We've already signed the documents."

Skyler grabbed one of the pews and clung onto it as the men tried to pull him from the room. "If you tell me that you were only doing your duty in healing me and that the feelings we shared were just part of the healing process, I'll leave."

"Wait!" Giada brought her hands to her forehead. Her breathing turned ragged as she lowered her hands.

The magistrate motioned for the men to release Skyler. Giada sought Alem's eyes for a brief moment. "I'm sorry." She raced to Skyler's open arms and laid her head on his chest. Skyler wrapped her in the warmth of his embrace. The blue light spilled around them as their pulses matched. Giada's heart reached out to him. She closed her eyes, as the Has'e bonding neared its pinnacle.

"Stop them!" Alem roared.

Too late. She couldn't end it even if she'd wanted to. Everything around them disappeared, all sound, all light, all smells, except for the caramel of the pomme on his breath and the brilliance of the cerulean glow surrounding them.

Alem gripped her arm as he yanked her away, ripping her from the sweet reverie. "You will *not* have her. She is *mine*. I paid for her!"

Giada pushed her hands against Alem's chest, struggling to free herself. Two security officers grabbed Skyler and shoved him to the back of the room.

"Enough!" the magistrate hollered over the din. The room grew silent. Mehlo went to his desk, picked up the digital and wiped the signatures off the marriage document. "When a Has'e bonds, there is no interfering. There can be no other marriage." He turned to Alem. "I'm sorry, my friend. There is nothing I can do."

Alem's face turned a darker shade as the fury of red covered his cheeks. He pointed at Skyler. "I'll see to it that you will not get one sina from me." He stormed from the room. The little man standing in the back followed him. The security officers released Skyler.

Giada flew to Skyler's embrace and pressed her cheek deeper into his flight suit as if she could penetrate his heart.

Skyler kissed the top of her head. "I never knew what it was like to give my heart so completely." He smoothed her cheek with his thumb then moved to her lips. "Please forgive me."

She reached up and wound her fingers in the curls at the nape of his neck. "You were paid to deliver me."

"I'm not sending my share back," Skyler said.

Giada pulled away from him. "Then I'm still bought and paid for."

"Not unless I give my share to my brother and his family." He drew her back to him. "And what about you? I thought you wanted to marry Alem Balek."

Giada gazed up into his eyes. "Only because I thought you cared more about the money."

Skyler groaned and pulled her against him, burying his fingers in her hair. "You have my heart."

"All right, we know you have each other's heart." The magistrate sounded irked. "Are you going to stand here and talk about your hearts all afternoon?"

"Will you marry us?" Skyler asked, then looked down at Giada. "That is what you want, since we already have each other's hearts?"

Giada nodded.

"Can we just get on with the marriage?" The magistrate cleared the screen of his digital "You are?"

"Skyler Rohn."

"Mr. Rohn, you press your hand here, and Ms. Hallspring – you know the routine."

Giada placed her palm over the signature section and Skyler did the same.

Mehlo closed the application. "Now you stand here and you here." He gave a quick motion to the spots where Giada and Alem had stood.

Skyler took both her hands in his. Giada couldn't take her gaze from his face as if trying to memorize every nuance of his features. The curls across his forehead hung in disarray. She wanted to reach up and play with them, to coil one around her finger.

"Since you're already bonded, all I need to say is you are now man and wife. I'd tell you to be good to each other, but that's pointless since I've never seen Has'e marriages fail – ever. Now go ahead and kiss each other." The magistrate left the room.

Breathless, Giada waited. Skyler pulled her against him, his arms holding her close as if he'd never let her go. Her arms wound around his neck. His mouth descended on hers. Giada wondered if she'd ever breathe again.

When he finally released her, she dropped her head to his chest, rejoicing in the rhythm that matched hers, now and forever. "For now, my heart. Tonight, all of me."

Skyler kissed her again. "Tomorrow we'll head back to Earth. I have some reparations to make there."

"And then I believe we must execute on a moon somewhere." Giada smiled up at him. It didn't matter where they went. They would always be together.

ABOUT THE AUTHOR

Betsy Love has loved to write from the moment she could hold a pen and has been creating stories since she was in elementary school. In high school, her creative writing teacher told her one day she would be published.

When not sitting at her computer pouring her heart and soul into her novels, she loves going to the high country and working on their property. But more than that, she loves spending time with her family. She is the mother of eight children and at last count she has 18 grandchildren. She pretends to garden and harvested five squash and 30 tomatoes last year. That may be a record.

If she had a horse, she'd ride it. If she had a pool she'd swim in it. But since she doesn't have either, she writes. She loves hanging out with her best friend, who happens to be her husband. He's been pretty darn amazing on her journey of publishing.

Connect with me online:
    Website: betsylove.com
    Email: authorbetsylove@gmail.com
    Facebook: Betsy Love-Author
    Twitter: @BetsyLoveAuthor
    Google+: BetsyLove

ACKNOWLEDGMENTS

First, and always, my gratitude goes to my Heavenly Father who gave me the gift of words. Second are my beta readers who helped me straighten out my words. Tici Smith and Gussie Fick were brutal! But that's exactly what my novel needed. Theresa Sneed, Stephanie Abney, Katie Teller and Nichole White helped me smooth out some rough spots. To Marsha Ward the founder of ANWA (American Night Writer's Association) who created a safe critique environment for writers and authors. Through our chapter meetings, they have helped me over the past several decades to hone my craft. My gratitude goes out especially to Ann Marie Jenner her amazing editing You ROCK! Last and certainly not least is my amazing husband who doesn't care if the house is a mess as long as I've been writing. I think I've finally convinced him that pajamas are an acceptable attire for my profession.

If you loved this book, please consider leaving a review! Authors live for your kind words.

BOOKS BY BETSY LOVE

Books by Betsy Love

The Healer's Heart

Falling for a Fraud

Surrogate Hearts

The Gravity of a Kiss

Identity

Soulfire

Plotting for Pantsers in 6 Easy Steps

The Miracle of Joie- A Sweetheart's Café Christmas Romance

Losing Grace

Young Adult Books by Lizzie Anne Love

*a*ka Betsy Love

The Penny Project

Mystic's Tale Series

The Dragon Keeper

COPYRIGHT

SNEAK PEAK-FALLING FOR A FRAUD

MAIL ORDER STARBRIDES-BOOK 2

CHAPTER 1

*K*at's stomach twisted in on itself as she tucked a lock of hair back into her braid. Not that it was going to stay put. She nudged her toes over the edge of the six-hundred-meter cliff. The team AeVe, Aero-vehicle, transport was barely a speck below Devil's Bluff. Closing her eyes, she bent her knees, spread her arms, and shot into the air.

The wind whirred in her ears so loudly that Kat couldn't even hear her inner voice telling her how foolish she was to jump without any safety protocols. She rolled onto her back and blew a kiss heavenward. "For you, Granddah." The sun smiled back at her through the polarized lenses of her goggles. She wished she could float up here, like this, forever.

As she turned back to face the ground, Kat focused on the transport where Hopsing waited for her. Soon, she'd be able to see her friend's bright pink hair, the signal to pull the rip cord. Before she spotted Hopsing, the pressure in her ears told her to release her chute. Kat ignored it, looking for land signals instead. Where did she go? If Kat had time, and her wrist digital, or WD, she'd have sent a communication to her.

The transport loomed larger, and still no Hopsing. Not only

should Kat have seen her best friend's bright pink hair, but her holo shirt with its geodesic design should be standing out bright against the landing pad, like a splash of lime on a blank canvas.

Narrowing her eyes, Kat searched the ground. She didn't have the luxury of waiting to spot her friend. She yanked the cord; the parasail snapped like her angry grandmother's apron and jerked Kat upward.

Floating to the ground on a soft cushion of air, Kat finally located Hopsing as she exited the transport—holding the altimeter and her WD.

"What were you thinking?" Hopsing squinted her brown eyes to slits as she held the device out to Kat. "You're going to get yourself hurt, or even killed. And if the enforcers had caught a glimpse of that stunt, that would have been your last jump."

"Yeah, I know." Kat's heart still beat with the thrill of free falling. Nobody understood the excitement of diving without protocols like she did, except Granddah. That's why she'd had to come clear out here, away from prying eyes.

She took the WD from Hopsing and attached it to her wrist. "Where were you, anyway? I was relying on seeing the top of your head so I'd know when to deploy." She dragged her parachute toward her, daisy chaining the cables to keep them from tangling.

Hopsing cringed. "You got a communication from Ai'bram on your WD that you left behind. That's when I found your altimeter. If I'd known you were going to pull such a stunt, I wouldn't have agreed to come with you."

Kat ignored the last remark. "You didn't tell Ai'bram where I was, did you?"

"No, of course not."

"What did he want?" Kat turned loose of the cables. A different kind of churning settled in her stomach as she hoped their captain hadn't gotten wind of what she had just done.

"What do you think?" Hopsing rolled her eyes. "It's always about money with him."

"I told him I'd take care of it." If it hadn't been for Tryst's careless-ness in their last exhibition, he wouldn't have gotten kicked off the team, and they wouldn't have lost their backers. As manager, it was up to Kat to find someone willing to risk their sinas on the team; an investor who wouldn't find out about Kat's solo jumping.

Hopsing shook the altimeter. "Keep doing stupid stuff like this and you'll get the whole team disqualified before regionals even start, with or without the funds." She hesitated, fear written across her face. She gave a nod toward the meadow. "I hope he's not an enforcer."

A man on a trail-runner floated toward them, kicking up fluffs of the baked dry grass behind him.

Kat hoisted the parachute toward the cables trying to hide the team's logo. No sense in getting everyone in trouble. "Guh! I thought you'd made sure no one else would be here today."

The man's blond hair didn't move against the wind, and he had a relaxed hold on the handle of his trail-runner. His smile showed brilliant white teeth as if he had them polished every day. As he came closer, his deep blue eyes picked up the color of the cloudless sky. He hopped off his trail-runner. "That was impressive."

Hopsing shot Kat a look, the color draining from her face.

"How so?" Kat blinked once at Hopsing, hoping she'd be able to play it cool, like jumping from Devil's Bluff was an everyday occurrence.

"Well, now, let's see; you jump from a cliff, not a Glouman, you have no hover-catch, no altimeter. Not many people display such a death-wish by jumping like that." His eyes never left her face.

"So, what are you going to do about it?" Kat continued to bunch up the parachute.

His smile left his face. "I'm not an enforcer, if that's what you were thinking." He held out his hand in introduction. "My friends call me Zo."

Kat didn't take his hand. Instead she made short work of unfastening her pack. "Your friends couldn't think of anything else? Zo, what shall we call you?"

Zo chuckled. "Zo, how was your day? Zo, what's the plan? Zo like you to do that." He arched his eyebrows. "I've heard them all. And well, yours was quite funny."

"I'll wait in the tranny while you sort this out." Hopsing slid into the back of the vehicle and ordered the window panels to darken.

Zo took his eyes off Kat. "Is she okay?"

"No, she's not." Kat smirked. "Even though she can jump from six kilometers in the air, Hopsing can't handle confrontational stalkers who appear out of nowhere."

"Confrontational?" Zo lifted his eyebrows.

"And a stalker." Kat dragged the chute to the storage compartment at the rear of the transport, careful so Zo couldn't see the team logo.

"I'm not stalking *her*." Zo smirked.

Kat's stomach sunk. "Oh, I see. Zo, you're stalking me."

"Well, not in the traditional sense."

She hit the fold button on the pack and the memory cables along with the chute retracted into the carry all.

Smiling, Zo arched one perfect, blond eyebrow and pointed at the chute. "It seems we have a lot in common."

"Apparently; you know a lot about jumping, the equipment, and protocols." Kat threw the pack into the storage compartment. "Are you a jumper?"

Zo leaned against the back of the transport. "Oh, no. I'll jump when pigs use hover-catches."

"So, what brings you out here...far away from civilization?"

"Can't a man enjoy a hike in the woods?" Zo squinted his blue eyes. Kat couldn't decide if that was from suspicion or the sun hitting him in the face.

"But you just said you were stalking." Kat pinched her lips. "I imagine you have a permit?"

Zo held out his WD with its holographic display. "Right here." He dropped his hand before Kat had a chance to examine the document. His gaze ran up her length and settled on her face. "Just as you have a jump permit?"

Kat closed the storage compartment. "Of course." However, she wasn't about to show him. If he wasn't an enforcer, and Ai'bram hadn't sent him, it was none of his business.

"And I suppose the Amahrians don't know you're jumping without following protocols?" His eyes sparkled with mischief. "No hover-catch." He pointed to her feet. The saucers which should have been attached to her ankles were absent. "And you're not wearing your altimeter. I believe your friend was holding it when you landed."

"Why are you spying on me?" Kat narrowed her eyes and stepped toward him. She was not going to be intimidated by this handsome man.

"Not spying, stalking." He held up a finger as if to correct her. "I was spying earlier."

"Zo, why are you stalking me?" She didn't care that he loomed over her, or that he smelled lightly of that heavenly fragrance, Pasha Vanille. She would ignore the fact that his good looks probably made other women's hearts melt. Granddah had warned her about men with pretty faces and hearts as shallow as diamond dust on Kalpathia.

Zo laughed. "I've heard so much about you, Katrina Cook, that I just had to meet you."

CHAPTER 2

*K*at took a step back, distrust flashed in her olive-green eyes. "How do you know my name?"

Lying had come too easy. It was part of Lorenzo's job, procuring starbrides for his associates off-world grooms. "You told me."

"No; no, I didn't." She shook her head and flipped her braid over her shoulder.

Kat was going to be a hard one to fool. He'd need much more planning than the last starbride he'd managed to lure. "You're right, of course. And you are also one incredibly intelligent young woman, just like your grandfather said you were."

Kat slammed the back of the transport and glared at him. "I don't know how you know my granddah, or why you're stalking me. Zo unless you have something more important to tell me…"

Lorenzo retreated a step. "Look, I'd just like to talk to you, and I certainly would never do anything to betray your grandfather's trust." In actuality, that was exactly what he intended to do. "Before your grandfather died—"

"What was my granddah's name?" Kat squinted her eyes in suspicion.

"Rhonan Cook."

"And tell me again how you know my granddah?"

Lorenzo gave a short huff. "Can we go somewhere and talk?"

"You come wallying out of the woods, spying on me."

"Stalking."

Her eyes flashed with anger. "Yes, that, too. And you expect me to just happily jaunt off with you somewhere like we're old pals?" She knocked on the door of the transport. The viewer cleared and Hopsing's face appeared behind the window. Kat gave a motion, signaling her to open the door.

He couldn't let her get away. "Please don't go. I have some important information for you." The last thing he needed to do was botch another job.

"I really have to go. My grandmah is expecting me for dinner." Kat reached for the security panel and the door slid open.

"Your grandfather didn't leave enough sinas for your jump team, did he? You've exhausted your resources and now you won't be able to make it to regionals unless you find a backer."

"You certainly seem to know so much about me." Kat clenched and unclenched her hands.

"I also know you solicited several backers and were turned down." Lorenzo pulled his mouth into a frown, and let his eyes droop. A show of sympathy. "I can help."

Kat didn't get in the transport as she pulled her hand from the panel and the door hissed closed on its hydraulics. "Really? How?"

Finally, he had her interest piqued. It wasn't quite the way he'd planned, but if she'd just hear him out. "What if I told you I found an investor who is familiar with your team, who's watched you for quite some time and wants to back the Elliptical Illusions."

Kat pressed her lips together, her focus flitting back and forth between the door and Lorenzo. "Go on."

Hopsing opened the door and slid out of the transport and stood next to Kat. "What kind of a backer?"

The phrasing had to be just right. "Someone who would have a much greater stake at losing than your team."

Hopsing took Kat's arm and whispered in her ear. "Do you think your grandfather trusts him? I mean, he never mentioned him." Lorenzo's hearing was better than most since his surgery.

"You're probably right." Kat slipped her hand over Hopsing's before turning to Lorenzo. "How does this backer know my grandfather?"

Lorenzo smiled, a lopsided one that looked stupid when he tried it in the mirror. Boyish, that's what his business associate, Elspeth, called it. She said it could melt a snowball in the Artic. "He's a very close friend of your grandfather." That was almost true.

"Oh, that clears things up. I'll sign right away." The sarcasm hung thick in her voice. "Why didn't my grandfather tell me about this before he died?"

He had to think fast. "There wasn't time to even tell your grandmother. With regionals coming up in less than a month, your grandfather knew you'd need a good backer. I've been watching the Ellipticals for quite some time. From what I've seen, you have a good shot at winning. It shouldn't really matter where the financing comes from. Can you trust that your grandfather had your best interest at heart?"

"If my grandfather had a backer, he would have told me. This isn't something he would have kept from me." Kat jerked out of Hopsing's hold.

"But—" Hopsing said.

Kat cut her off. "Get in the tranny."

"Because the backer wished to remain anonymous." He retrieved one of his business cards and held it out to Kat. "Think about it, and if you'd like more information, you can contact me."

She didn't reach for it. Hopsing tapped on the glass and nodded for her to take it.

While Lorenzo had watched her from a distance and had always wanted to talk to her, he had no idea that she'd leave him fumbling like a confused referee in an aerial soccer game.

He would have to figure out another way to get her to listen.

CHAPTER 3

*K*at bit the skin on the side of her nail, the one that she always managed to catch when she pulled the ripcord. If it hadn't been for Zo interrupting her jubilation, today's jump would have been perfect, even if it might be one of her last.

Hopsing sat beside her in the front seat and programmed in their destination, then thumbed through her WD. "I can't find anything on Zo."

"Of course, you wouldn't. How many Zos are there?" Kat stared out the window watching the steep canyon walls pass by. Rubbing her temples, she tried to banish the pain that had taken up residence there.

Hopsing closed out of her WD and clasped her hands in her lap. "Would it hurt for you to at least hear him out?"

Kat wrinkled her nose and bit her lip. "Don't you find it odd that someone who supposedly knows my granddah comes wallying out of the forest like he's all chummy with me? I don't know whether he knows Granddah or not."

"Well, he certainly can't be after your money." Hopsing chuckled. "It's not like your grandfather left you with a lot." She turned in her seat and faced Kat directly. "What if he's like this talent scout who goes around looking for people he can invest in. What if he's filthy rich, and because your granddah made you focus on your jumping, this Zo guy couldn't get close enough for you to get to know him."

"No, that doesn't sound right." Although every guy who'd ever tried to get close to Kat ended up on the dark side of the moon shoveling asteroid dust—Hopsing had a point. That couldn't be it, either. Her granddah would have somehow gotten word to Grandmah. Unless she didn't want her granddaughter jumping any more. That had to be it.

Kat leaned her head back against the seat. "As soon as I get home, I'm going to ask my grandmah if she's heard of this Zo guy. She'd never out-and-out lie to me about something like this."

Once they reached Kat's home, she stepped from the transport and waved to Hopsing. "I'll see you Friday."

The transport hovered off along the lower magnetic trac. Kat smiled when she looked up at her home. With its modifications, like the receding roof over the bedrooms, and the kinetic front door, the house still looked odd among the high-rise buildings and modern technology. Granddah had insisted Grandmah enjoy the comforts of technology—an odd conglomeration of 2250 AD meets the future.

Gran waited on the front porch of the three-hundred-year-old house. She wrung her hands before running her palm over her red hair with its single streak of gray. "Katie, my precious." Gran hurried down the steps and embraced her as if Kat had been gone longer than a few hours.

Kat always loved her grandmother's arms as they enfolded her, wrapping her like the comforter Gran had made for her, using the old art form called quilting. Kat pressed her cheek against the older woman's soft, wrinkled face, drawing strength from her warmth. "God between us and all harm," she whispered in Gran's ear.

"'Tis I always worry when you go jumping." Her rough voice spoke in Kat's ear.

"'Tis I always worry when you wring your hands Zo—I mean so." Kat kept her face buried in her grandmother's embrace for fear Gran would see the color that had flamed to her cheeks at the slip of that man's name. His blue eyes shining in the sunlight, his shirt pulled tight across his muscles and his self-assured gait. No, she would not allow herself to be pulled in by surface handsome. She'd hold out for a man with a beautiful heart, just like her gran had done.

About that beautiful man. "Grandmah, before Granddah died, did he mention a backer for the jump team?"

Grandmah released her and headed into the house without looking at Kat. "Come inside."

Kat followed her grandmah into the warm kitchen. The aroma of baked bread filled the cozy room. Kat wished Gran would use the food replicator to save not only her spare sinas, but her strength as well; however, Kat had to admit that no replicator bread ever tasted like her grandmah's.

Gran sliced the loaf and set the slices on a plate. "Now, Katie, my girl, sit and tell me about your jump today, lest I worry something horrible happened."

"Did you not hear my question?" Kat sat at the table and waited.

Gran set the plate on the Battenberg lace cloth and buttered a thick slice of bread. "I heard you. First you tell me about your jump."

Zo was right. Granddah had made arrangements. "It was well."

"Well? Is that all you can say?" Gran took Kat's chin and gazed into her eyes. "You usually have so much more to tell. Who sucked the wind out of you today?"

"Zo."

"So what?" Grandmah handed the slice to Kat.

"No, Zo—that's the name of the man who said he knew Granddah and that Granddah found an investor for our team." Kat took the bread and breathed in the buttery aroma before taking a large bite. The flavor of yeast filled her senses.

Grandmah pinched her lips, rolling them into a thin line. "I told him it was a bad idea. Told him not to trust a man just because he talks pretty."

Kat swallowed. "Why didn't you tell me about him?"

"Because the man backed out."

Wiping at the spots of butter on the corner of her mouth, Kat said,

"Today, he met me at the jump site and is willing to invest."

Grandmah frowned, and her eye-wrinkles deepened. "Hmm...I told your granddah it was a mistake."

"Do you know him?" Kat sank her teeth into another warm bite.

"No, and your granddah didn't know him that well either." Grandmah set another piece in front of Kat, before wringing her hands again. She stood and went to the window overlooking her garden. "The historical committee called again."

"You told them no, right?" Kat slathered butter onto the new piece.

Grandmah turned, deep wrinkles creasing her brow. "If it was only that simple."

"Do you want me to talk to them?" Kat asked between bites as she chewed.

Grandmah didn't answer her right away. She picked up the remaining half of the loaf and set it in a storage container, then returned to the table. "No, this is for me alone to tackle." She slumped into the seat opposite Kat.

"Now about that investor. Did he approach you?" Clearly Grandmah did not want to talk about her worries. It was so like her to not want to trouble Kat. She wished her gran would let her help more.

"Yes, while I was at my jump. What do you think I should do?" Kat asked.

A deep scowl spread across Gran's face. "I don't like it. 'Tis why I never told you. Especially after the man backed out. I just don't trust him. You know I don't particularly care for your jumping, but it makes you happy. I would never keep you from that."

Kat finished the last bite and stood. "But?"

Moisture sprung up in Gran's eyes. "I couldn't bear it if I lost you."

Gathering her grandmother in her arms, Kat couldn't help the niggling of guilt, knowing she'd jumped without safety protocols, and knowing she'd almost not deployed her chute in time. "I'll be careful." Next time, she'd use her altimeter, even if it detracted from the thrill. Without Kat, Grandmah would never make it financially. Now, if their team could win Globals, that would ensure her grandmah's comfort for the rest of her life.

CHAPTER 4

*L*orenzo stood outside his business associate's apartment and studied her name plate.

Elspeth Montgomery
Procurer of Oddities and Commodities

He hesitated before he chimed his arrival. His report, while not terrible, was not going to be what she wanted to hear. Since the debacle with the last bride, he had to make sure this one went smoothly. He prided himself on being able to deliver the *goods*.

One advantage of Ms. Cook's grandfather keeping his grand-daughter isolated was that she had no hopefuls; men who would distract her. Rhonan had done a great job of keeping her focused on her career. Not that Lorenzo intended on pretending to be her hopeful, especially after their exchange. Kat would be a hard one to woo. Not only was she quick-witted, but deeply intelligent as well. Her flashing green eyes set against her fair, freckled skin, and coppery red hair would certainly be an added dividend. The man who'd procured their services had specific requirements. Kat fit them perfectly, right down to her feisty temperament.

Lorenzo pressed the chime on the recognition panel and waited.

The door whooshed open. Elspeth stood with a cup in her hand, steam wafting into the air. "It's about time." She motioned for him to enter and led him to a high-back chair. "Yousa?"

"Yes, please." Lorenzo hung his jacket on the antiquated coatrack. He found it fascinating that a woman as youthful as his associate chose to live and dress like someone living in the early nineteen-hundreds, especially in a modern building with all its state-of-the-art conveniences.

Elspeth returned with another mug and handed it to Lorenzo. Her bustled dress crinkled as she sank onto her brocade couch. With a confident hand, she smoothed her chestnut-colored hair as if a single strand dared to escape the piles of curls atop her head. "How did your meeting with Katrina Cook go?"

He took a sip, the flavor rich against his tongue. "Rather well, considering."

"Considering what?" Elspeth set her cup on the coaster on the table.

Besides her grandfather not introducing Lorenzo before he died, or that the other backer had withdrawn his offer after Rhonan's death, his first introduction had produced quite a spark between them. Lorenzo looked forward to meeting with her again.

"Lorenzo?" Elspeth raised her eyebrows.

"Sorry; was trying how to best describe our meeting." Lorenzo set his cup on the table.

"Coaster." She placed a matching disc under his mug. "Go on."

Lorenzo settled into the chair and ran his hand along the floral brocade fabric. "Katrina Cook is everything that Haysel Laene will adore. She's probably the most beautiful red-head I've ever met. She's witty and rather charming."

Elspeth leaned forward. "Don't tell me what she's like. Did she agree to the terms?"

Closing his eyes, he sought for the right words. "Not yet," was all he could come up with.

"Not yet? What do you mean, not yet?" Elspeth shot out of her chair, bumping the table and toppling her mug. Her Whirr flew from the wall and sucked up the liquid, then ran a polisher over the surface.

Lorenzo picked at a piece of lint and took it off his tailored pants. "What I meant was, we're going to meet later for the terms. In the meantime, her interest is piqued."

Elspeth crossed to her desk. "I have something to show you."

Lorenzo retrieved his yousa, which had not suffered Elspeth's frustration, and followed her into her office space and stood beside her, eyeing images of several Earther men displayed on her desktop hologram.

"Quite a few requests have come in this morning." She motioned to one of the men. "Since I already have some women who have agreed to be brides, it's simply a matter of matching them up according to their compatibility." She pulled up another hologram of a woman and set her image next to one of the Earthers. "I can take care of these. You shouldn't have any trouble doing what you do best—convincing Ms. Cook to join the ranks of eligible bachelorettes." With deft motions she paired the images of the men with the women, leaving one man without a match. Haysel Laene.

Elspeth drummed her manicured fingers on her antique desk. "I've received a communication from Mr. Laene earlier today. He is most anxious to meet Katrina." Placing a hand on her corseted waist, she turned to Lorenzo, and rested one hip against the desk. "He arrives at the end of the month and expects his bride to be primed and waiting for him. The marriage will take place on Earth before they head back to Kyrea."

"That only gives me three weeks." Lorenzo ran his hand over his hair, then jerked it away. It had taken him too long to get those stubborn curls to lay flat. "That doesn't give me much time."

Elspeth gave him one of her mischievous smiles. "Then perhaps you should get to it."

He took her hand and gave it a squeeze. "It pays a debt…." He couldn't finish. In the first four years, he'd loved his new face and the power it gave him. In the last year, he'd tried to convince himself he was doing this because of Elspeth's generosity. If it hadn't been for her, he'd be dead, or at the very least living an invalid's life.

Lorenzo took his coat off the rack and headed for the door. He stopped before leaving. "You are amazing at matching couples—helping them find love. I'm sure there are other marriage brokers who could not do what you do." Lorenzo paused. "Perhaps you should think about a match for you. Then perhaps you might be able to find peace."

She pressed a shaky hand over her abdomen. "Most of my grooms want a woman to carry on their blood lines. I suppose if I could...."

Lorenzo leaned on the door jam and eyed the fedora that had belonged to her late husband. "Maybe if you'd given him your whole heart, you'd have freed yourself to have children."

A wistful smile crossed her face. "If he'd lived longer we might have—I might have...." The thought trailed off and Elspeth went back to her usual business self. "Katrina is the perfect match. I'm sure you can find a way to secure her interest."

www.ingramcontent.com/pod-product-compliance
Lightning Source LLC
Chambersburg PA
CBHW060922180626
46817CB00004B/1352